Praise for *Nichole Severn*

"First-class romantic suspense! *Rules in Blackmail* will keep you reading late into the night!"
—*New York Times* bestselling author Cynthia Eden

"Action-packed from the first chapter to the last! Smart heroine. Sexy hero. *Rules in Rescue* has it all."
—*USA TODAY* bestselling author Janie Crouch

"With action from page one, *Rules in Deceit* is a breathtaking, non-stop ride full of romance and suspense!"
—*USA TODAY* bestselling author Rachel Grant

"Fast-paced, explosive action makes Nichole Severn's *Rules in Defiance* an exciting, romantic read!"
—*New York Times* bestselling author Toni Anderson

CAUGHT IN THE CROSSFIRE

—

NICHOLE SEVERN

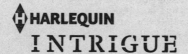

This is for you! This series wouldn't keep going without you.

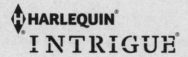

ISBN-13: 978-1-335-13674-9

Caught in the Crossfire

Copyright © 2020 by Natascha Jaffa

Recycling programs
for this product may
not exist in your area.

This edition published by arrangement with Harlequin Books S.A.

For questions and comments about the quality of this book,
please contact us at CustomerService@Harlequin.com.

Harlequin Enterprises ULC
22 Adelaide St. West, 40th Floor
Toronto, Ontario M5H 4E3, Canada
www.Harlequin.com

Printed in U.S.A.

Nichole Severn writes explosive romantic suspense with strong heroines, heroes who dare challenge them and a hell of a lot of guns. She resides with her very supportive and patient husband, as well as her demon spawn, in Utah. When she's not writing, she's constantly injuring herself running, rock climbing, practicing yoga and snowboarding. She loves hearing from readers through her website, www.nicholesevern.com, and on Twitter, @nicholesevern.

Books by Nichole Severn

Harlequin Intrigue

Blackhawk Security

Rules in Blackmail
Rules in Rescue
Rules in Deceit
Rules in Defiance
Caught in the Crossfire

Midnight Abduction

Visit the Author Profile page at Harlequin.com.

CAST OF CHARACTERS

Kate Monroe—As Blackhawk Security's resident profiler, she's more than prepared to hunt the monsters hiding in the darkest shadows, but her first assignment since returning from leave quickly becomes more than she can handle when her past catches up to her.

Declan Monroe—The former special agent can't remember anything before waking up in the hospital with four bullets in his chest. Not even the wife he left behind. But now that a serial killer has put Kate in his sights, Declan's more determined than ever to recover his memories—and his marriage.

Ryan Dominguez—A rising star in the FBI's Behavior Analysis Unit, Special Agent Ryan Dominguez has been a close personal friend of Kate's since her husband—his former partner—was murdered. And he'll do anything to keep her safe. Even if it means saving her from herself.

The Hunter—Serial killer who stalks, seduces and kills his victims by setting them free in the wilderness before hunting them down and shooting an arrow through their hearts.

Blackhawk Security—Comprised of an elite team of specialists with diverse backgrounds ranging from former Special Forces to psychology, Blackhawk Security offers personal protective services for people whose lives are endangered.

Chapter One

Your husband is alive, Kate.

Blackhawk Security profiler Kate Monroe stared at her reflection in the broken picture frame on the floor. Had it really been an entire year? She hadn't set foot in this house since the ambush, too traumatized to pull the bullets out of the walls, too sentimental to put it on the market. Everything had changed that night.

Tightening her grip on the manila folder in her hand, she couldn't ignore the truth. Declan hadn't died as she'd been told while recovering in the hospital from her own injuries. He'd survived. He'd disappeared. And he'd left her behind.

Glass crunched under her shoes, bringing her back into the moment, and the photo came into focus. Her and Declan dancing at their wedding, surrounded by smiling guests.

Burying the burn behind her sternum deeper, she stepped over the frame. Blackhawk's private investigator had found proof—a timestamped photo—of Declan taken a month ago in downtown Anchorage.

She'd stared at it for hours, picked it apart pixel by pixel to fight the anger and resentment bubbling up her throat. In vain. The photo was real. Declan was alive, and she deserved to know why he hadn't come home.

There had to be something here that would lead her to his location. Setting the folder on what was left of the kitchen table, she fought back the memories of hundreds of dinners as she dragged her fingers over the bullet-riddled surface. She pulled out drawers in the kitchen, emptied the bookshelf beside the desk Declan had built for her, scattered old patient files across the carpet.

Bending to pick them up, Kate froze as the dark stains at her feet came into focus. Blood. Ice worked through her veins. She couldn't think—couldn't breathe. She closed her eyes against the memories fighting to rush forward and forced herself to take a deep breath. She'd been a psychologist. She'd helped others through their trauma—their pain— why couldn't she get past her own?

She traced over one mound of scar tissue below her collarbone, leaving the files where they fell. Swallowing against the tightness in her throat, she straightened. Gunshot wounds never healed. Not really. Six months since the last surgery, and the physical pain from three shots to the chest still lingered. Then again, she'd been lucky to survive at all. The gunman who'd opened fire on her and Declan hadn't meant to leave anyone alive.

Movement registered off to her right and she automatically reached for the Glock in her shoulder holster. Depressing the safety tab, she took aim, heart in her throat. Blackhawk Security's founder and CEO insisted his agents trained in wilderness survival, weapons, hostage negotiation, recovery and rescue and more, but she was a profiler. Not former military like Anthony. Not a former NSA consultant like Elizabeth. She'd never had use for a gun.

Her hands shook slightly as the weight of heavy steel threatened to pull her arms down. She'd never aimed her gun at another human being. "You're trespassing on private property," she said. "Come out with your hands where I can see them, and I promise not to shoot you."

The house had been abandoned for a year. Wasn't hard to imagine the homeless taking advantage of a roof over their heads, and she wasn't interested in forcing them to leave if that was the case. The house wasn't going anywhere. It took everything she had to stay here this long.

Shadows shifted across the intruder's features, and her breath caught in her throat. Hints of moonlight highlighted the familiar shape of his stubbled jaw, his broad chest, muscled arms and short blond hair. Her heart beat hard as she stood there, unsure if he was real or a figment of her imagination.

He closed the distance between them slowly, cautiously, as though he believed she might actually shoot him. She couldn't make out the color of his eyes in the darkness but pictured the ice-blue depths clearly from memory as he stared back at her.

"It's you." She suppressed the sob clawing up her throat but couldn't fight the burn against her lower lash line. Rushing forward, Kate wrapped her arms around his broad chest, his clean, masculine scent working deep into her lungs. A year. A year he'd put her through hell. The grief, the anger. Why hadn't he reached out to her? Who had she buried all those months ago? Why wasn't he hugging her back?

Clenching her teeth to keep the scream at bay, Kate backed off but didn't holster the weapon. Why was he just standing there? "Say something."

"You're even more beautiful than I remembered." That voice. His voice.

An electric sizzle caught her nerve endings on fire and exploded throughout her entire system. She never thought she'd hear that voice again.

Declan Monroe shifted closer, the weight of his gaze pressurizing the air in her lungs. "You don't need the gun. I'm not going to hurt you."

"That's all you're going to say to me?" It felt as if someone had driven a fist into her stomach. "You've been alive this whole time, and that's all you're going to say? They told me you died in that hospital. I—" The pain of that day, of losing her best friend, of losing the man she'd intended to spend the rest of her life with, the man she'd planned on starting a family with, surged to the surface. "I buried you."

"I can't imagine what you've been through." He reached out, smoothed his fingertips down her jawline. Even with the ice of shock coursing through her, warmth penetrated deep into her bones, but his expression kept her from reveling in his missed touch.

Declan lowered his hand as he studied the aftermath in the living room. The bullet holes in the walls, the broken picture frames, the destroyed sectional and cushions. She didn't have the guts to see what'd become of the rest of the house, a home that was once their safe haven from their dark careers. "Is this where it happened?"

Confusion gripped her hard, and Kate narrowed her eyes to see his face. "What do you mean—"

"I get these flashes sometimes. Of this house, of different things." Declan motioned to his head, then his gaze locked back on her. "Mostly of you. Some days it's glimpses, other times I can see you so clearly walking through that front door with stacks of files in your arms and a smile on your face. Like it was real."

Her head jerked to the side of its own accord slightly as though she'd been slapped. Instinct screamed. This wasn't right. She took a step back, the gun still in her hand.

"But I still don't know your name," he said.

Air rushed from her lungs. She struggled to keep upright as the world tilted on its axis.

Strong hands steadied her before she hit the bloodstained floor a second time, but the gun slipped from her hold. Leveraging her weight against the desk, she pushed back stray hairs that had escaped from the low bun at the base of her neck. She had to breathe. Her pulse beat hard at the base of her throat as his hand slipped down her spine.

How could he have forgotten her name? Every cell in her body rejected the idea her husband had been walking around Anchorage without the slightest clue he'd been married, had a life, had a job. Where had he been all this time?

"You okay?" He was still touching her. Even through the thick fabric of her cargo jacket, she'd recognize those familiar strokes. "I'll get you some water."

"No." The city had probably turned off the water a long time ago. She'd been paying the mortgage on the house in addition to the rent on her small apartment, but utilities would've been a waste. Kate maneuvered out of his reach. "I'm fine. I…need some air."

Lie. Nothing about the situation, about the fact the husband she'd lost was standing in front of her, was fine. Fresh air wouldn't do a damn bit of good.

Space. She needed space. The home they'd shared for more than half a decade blurred in her peripheral vision as she headed for the front door. Debris and remnants of their life together threatened to trip her up, but she wouldn't stop until there was at least two inches of door between them. Couldn't.

The cold Alaskan night prickled goose bumps along her arms as she closed the door behind her. She set the crown of her head against the wood, pressing her shoulders into the door. One breath. Two. She kept counting until she mentally reached ten.

None of this made sense. His surgeon had told her Declan hadn't survived the shooting. That he'd done everything he could to save her husband, but nothing worked. Declan had lost too much blood, the bullets had torn through major arteries and nobody could've saved him.

No wonder he'd suggested she take the time to heal from her own wounds before identifying the body. It hadn't been to save her from seeing her husband on a slab. It'd been to cover his mistake. By the time she'd had the strength to get out of that damn bed, it'd been too late. The hospital had released who she thought had been her husband into her custody, and Declan's former partner had taken responsibility for all of the funeral arrangements. Had anyone but the surgeon known her husband hadn't been inside that coffin?

The surgeon had lied. Why?

She swiped at her face as the tears finally fell. Declan didn't know her name?

Tires screeched on asphalt a few houses down. Headlights flared to life, but she couldn't see the driver through the truck's windshield. Probably one of the neighbor's teenagers. It'd been so long since she'd lived on this street, she didn't know who had moved away after the shooting, her new neighbors' names or if any of them had kids old enough to drive.

Wasn't important. Staying calm long enough to

assess the situation, that was all that mattered now. The engine revved loud in her ears as the faint outline of the passenger-side window lowered.

The door supporting her disappeared, and strong hands pulled her inside a split second before the first bullet of many shattered through the house's main window. Kate hit the floor hard, her head snapping back as Declan returned fire. She checked her holster—empty—and recognized the gun in his hand. Her Glock.

The sound of pealing tires faded, and the gunfire ceased.

Declan barricaded them inside the house, his back to the front door as he dropped the gun's magazine, counted the rounds left and slammed it back into place. Apparently there were some things amnesia couldn't destroy, loading a weapon being one of them.

Light blue eyes settled on her as he offered her his hand. Calluses slid against her palms as he wrapped his hand around hers and pulled her into him. "Are you hurt?"

"I'm getting tired of people shooting at me." Her awareness of him hiked to an all-time high. The pounding of his heartbeat against her palm, the pressure of his attention on her. Even the way he held her took a bit of the strength out of her knees.

She shook her head and stepped out of his reach to counteract the heat rising in her neck. He'd saved her life. The least she could do was help him recover his. "It's Kate, by the way. My name is Kate."

KATE.

That name was perfect for the blonde beauty with the shadows in her gaze. Striking green eyes, eyes that had haunted his memories for over a year, narrowed in on him. Thinner than he remembered from his memory's brief flashes of her, she shook his insides like the earthquake that hit Japan and brought down the nuclear reactors, leaving him breathless and full at the same time. A T-shirt and jeans hugged her athletic form, her frame hidden by an oversized green cargo jacket. But he knew every curve, every scar, every valley and ridge of muscle from memory.

The realization he hadn't gone crazy after waking up alone in a hospital room settled his nerves. He hadn't imagined her. Hadn't imagined this house. From what he'd been able to tell, they'd lived here. Together.

The real-life sight of her was enough to help him forget he'd just taken a bullet.

He let go of the gun, the crash of metal on hardwood loud in his ears, as his strength drained drop by drop. The driver had fishtailed out of the neighborhood a few seconds ago. No telling if that bastard would circle around for another shot at her, but adrenaline was already leaving his system. He was losing blood. Fast.

"Declan?" Those mesmerizing green eyes shot to his side as his shirt soaked through. "You've been shot."

Declan Monroe. That was his name. Not the one he'd adopted over the last year.

Her attention dulled the pain in his side. He'd find the SOB who'd taken a shot at her. He couldn't remember a damn thing about his life before waking up in that hospital bed, but he'd remembered her. She was important enough for his brain to hang on to, and he'd sure as hell do what he had to to keep her safe.

Blood spread across his T-shirt faster than he thought possible. "Isn't that supposed to stay inside my body?"

"Bullets tend to have other ideas. Lie down. I need to look at the wound," she said.

So levelheaded. So rational. She'd been shot at and now had to inspect a bullet wound. How was she able to keep this calm?

He clamped a hand over his side and stumbled as the pain reared its ugly head, but Kate kept him from collapsing to the floor when the dizziness took control. Her fingers brushed against his oversensitive skin, and a jolt of awareness chased the nerves up his arm and into his chest. The flashlight from her phone blinded him. Swiping her tongue across her bottom lip as she knelt beside him, she holstered the weapon without meeting his gaze. Had she felt it, too? The invisible pull urging him to touch her?

Lifting his shirt, she paused. "I need some hydrogen peroxide and towels to see past the blood. Don't move."

It'd taken him a year to get here, inside this

house, to her. He wasn't going to lose her now. He forced himself to straighten. "No. That shooter could come back any minute to make sure he's finished the job. I'm getting you out of here."

"Big words from the man bleeding out on my floor. You're not going anywhere. At least, not until I see how bad it is." Setting her hand over his chest, she pushed him flat onto the floor. Kate disappeared from his side, everything inside of him aware of the space between them.

He focused on the sound of shifting debris and the slamming of cabinets to distract himself. In less than a minute, she crouched beside him with a stack of towels and a bottle of whiskey. "This is all I could find. If you move, you're going to wish you were really were dead."

I buried you. Her words echoed through his head.

"You know what happened to me." None of the flashbacks had revealed that particular memory. Before she stepped foot in the house, he'd gone through most of the paperwork stashed in the desk for leads, each folder detailing therapy notes by Dr. Kate Monroe, a psychologist. He'd studied the holes in the walls, the broken picture frames, the destroyed personal effects. But nothing had triggered another memory.

"You were ambushed." After dousing her hands in the whiskey, she prodded at the sides of the bullet wound. Her fingers feathered over his skin, cooling the fire spreading through his pain receptors. "One of my patients became obsessed with me, and when he discovered he couldn't have me, he decided no one should. You were caught in the cross fire."

"There are pictures of us together. I remember you." He hissed as she poured the alcohol over the hole in his side. Stinging agony rippled through him, and he fought to catch his breath. He might've been shot, but he'd gone an entire year without knowing who he was, where he came from, who he'd left behind. "Who am I to you?"

Using one of the towels she collected from the kitchen, she applied pressure to the wound. Still refusing to look at him. She reached for another towel. "We can't stop the bleeding while the bullet is inside. We need to get you to a hospital."

Anxiety accelerated his pulse. The last hospital he'd set foot inside had kept him fully stocked with enough nightmare material to last him a lifetime. Waking up alone. Four holes in his body. Not knowing who he was. There was no way in hell he was going back for another round.

"No hospitals." Declan wrapped one hand onto her forearm, and her attention snapped to his. His heart rate slowed, the pain disappearing as time seemingly stood still. He noted the slight change in her expression, the furrow between her brows deeper than a moment ago. He blinked to counteract the darkness closing in around the edges of his vision. "You have to get the bullet out."

"I'm a profiler for a security firm." She tried pulling out of his grip, but he only held her tighter. The tension between her neck and shoulders visibly strained. "I never went to medical school. I'm not a trained medical doctor—"

"I trust you, Kate." And he meant it. Every word. Because even though he'd lost his memories from before he woke up in that hospital bed alone, something deep inside knew her as well as his body knew how to breathe. He couldn't explain it. Didn't need a reason why or how. She'd left enough of an impression that his own brain couldn't get rid of her as it had everything else, and he wasn't about to give that up. Despite the mysterious circumstances surrounding how he'd ended up in that hospital in the first place. "You can do this."

She studied him. "Blackhawk Security has a doctor on staff. She can help—"

"No." He growled. "It has to be you."

"Remember that when you bleed out all over the floor." The tightness drained from her shoulders as she shifted her weight between both knees. She swiped the back of her hand across her face. "Okay. If we're going to do this, I need to find something sharp enough to widen the wound so I can extract the bullet. Hopefully, it's still in one piece."

He set his jaw against another surge of pain and replaced her hand with his own for pressure to slow the bleeding. She disappeared deeper into the house.

His heart pounded loud behind his ears, a slow, rhythmic beat that made his eardrums ache. The seconds ticked by, maybe a minute. They were running out of time.

When she came back, her phone's flashlight

beam highlighted her supplies beside him. He used every last bit of strength to focus on her as she gently removed the towel.

"Are you sure about this?" she asked.

He nodded, quick and curt, the words stuck in his throat with the weight of pain squeezing the air in his lungs.

"Okay. Then no matter what happens," she said, "I need you to hold still."

Sirens echoed. One of the neighbors must've called the police. Cops meant ambulances, questions he couldn't answer and hospitals.

"What's one more scar, right?" She was trying to distract him, keep him focused on the present when all he wanted to do was compare the woman in front of him to the memories in his head. He'd noticed his own scars, of course, the mounds of tissue peppered across his abdominals, and from the slight dip of her neckline, he recognized a similar mass peeking out from beneath her shirt. Did that mean...

"Declan?" she asked.

"Who did that to you?" Rage—pure and hot—engulfed him, pushed the fact that someone had put a hole in him to the back of his mind. Someone had shot her. Too fast, too hard, the crack in his control started to spread as he imagined her lying in one of those bloodstains on the carpet in the dining room. Who the hell shot her? He'd tear them apart with his bare hands. He'd find the bastard and make him pay, just as he'd find the one who'd tried a few minutes ago.

Another dose of adrenaline and pain drove him to try to sit up. A dangerous combination with a gunshot wound. The quicker his heart beat, the quicker he'd bleed out.

"Declan, you have to stay still." Setting her palms against him, she struggled to keep him in place. "The bullet is too deep. If I keep digging, I could permanently damage something or kill you, and I'm not willing to take either of those chances. We have to get you to the hos—"

"No hospitals." Black spiderwebs snaked across his vision, and suddenly he didn't have the strength to keep himself upright. He collapsed back against the tile. Damn it. He'd lost too much blood.

"Fine, but you need a doctor. Blackhawk Security keeps one on site." Dim lighting illuminated her face as she raised her phone to her ear, and he blinked against the sudden brightness of her phone's screen. Her exhale brushed across his neck as she smoothed her hand across his forehead. "Anthony, track my location. I need an evacuation. Adult male, gunshot wound to the left side. I can't stop the bleeding."

No emotion in her voice or on her expression. Too clinical. Too rational. That wasn't the woman he remembered. Or had the flashbacks of her been a lie all this time?

"ETA?" Kate nodded, that brilliant green gaze

he'd dreamed about for months centering on him. "See you in ten minutes."

"You never answered my question from before." He closed his eyes for a moment. Forget the bullet. There was only one thing that mattered. He leveraged his heels into the floor and forced himself to sit straighter against the front door. Pressure released on the wound, and he could breathe a bit easier. His fingertips tingled with the urge to touch her, but a hollowness had set up residence in his gut at the sound of her emotionless conversation with someone named Anthony. Maybe they hadn't been as close as he thought after all? Maybe he'd imagined everything. "Who am I to you?"

Kate wiped the back of her hand across her forehead again. A nervous habit?

"Everything that happened the night you died was my fault," she said. "I didn't take his threats seriously. I didn't think he'd—" The flashlight from her phone streaked across her face as she turned her phone over in her free hand. And there it was. A chink in that self-controlled armor. "My patient came to the house that night because you're—you *were*—my husband."

Chapter Two

Every wound had shaped her, forced her to become a stronger version of the woman she'd been before the ambush. No one was 100 percent safe. No matter how hard she tried—no matter how much she needed—to repress the fear, the uncertainty, it barged straight back into her life the moment that single bullet tore a hole through her husband's body.

Kate ran a hand through her hair as she paced Blackhawk Security's main hall for the tenth—or was it the eleventh? —time.

Declan's body. They weren't married anymore. Once he'd been declared dead, their marriage had ended, but she couldn't lose him. Not again. She'd barely survived the first time. Having him here, alive, almost well, had given her hope. She'd been alone for so long, broken for so long, she didn't know what to do now. Should she be in there with him, standing by his side as the doctor removed the bullet and stitched him up?

"Who shot at you tonight?" Anthony Harris, Blackhawk Security's weapons expert, had planted himself against a wall and watched her wear a path in the firm's brand-new carpet.

As a former Ranger, he only cared about one thing: protecting the people he cared about. Once upon a time, that short list had only included their team: Sullivan Bishop, founder and CEO of Blackhawk; Vincent Kalani, their forensics expert; Elizabeth Dawson headed network security; Elliot Dunham, the best private investigator and the reason she was standing here at all; and her.

But now, Anthony had a family. A wife, a son. Yet he'd come within minutes of Kate's evacuation request. He was reliable. Solid. And terrifying behind those aviator sunglasses he wore 24/7. She'd shut down the urge to profile her teammates, but she had read his file. Within moments of meeting him for the first time, she understood he strapped himself with as many weapons as he could because he feared losing his support system like he had in Afghanistan. War changed people—made them desperate—and Anthony hadn't been any different.

Kate slowed her pace, released the breath she'd been holding. Her scars burned, but the sensation was only in her head. She knew that. The adrenaline lingering in her veins from the situation—almost the exact same one she'd survived a year ago—was her brain's way of protecting her. Of sending up a warning. Besides, it'd been months since her last surgery, and scar tissue lacked nerve cells. She wasn't supposed to feel anything.

She studied the small window in the door leading

to the firm's medical suite, and her insides tightened. She wasn't supposed to feel at all.

"I have no idea who pulled the trigger tonight." The shooting couldn't have been a coincidence. The chances both she and Declan would be in that house again, at the same time... There were too many variables to calculate. Especially given that Declan Monroe had legally died over a year ago. Had he been waiting for her to show? Brian Michaels, her patient who destroyed everything she'd known in the span of a minute, was still behind bars. Whoever had shot at them tonight couldn't have been him. Why come after her now? Or had she been the target at all?

"Take it easy on the carpet, Doc." Anthony pushed off the wall, hands dropping to his sides for better access to his arsenal if necessary. "Sullivan will kill you if he has to pay to replace it twice in two months."

Right. The bomb meant for their network security analyst had wiped out this entire floor two months ago. Was that her teammate's way of telling her they were never safe, even in the most protected and secure building in Anchorage?

Blackhawk Security employed the finest security experts in the world. She and her team provided personal protection, private investigating, logistical support to the US government, profiling and personal recovery. Whatever their client needed, they delivered. They did it all, and they did a good job. If the shooter had been targeting her, he'd be insane to try here.

Kate slowed her pacing, fingers tightening into fists. She was losing her mind. She was better than this. She'd been a psychologist. She'd struggled through months of grief by shutting everything down, ignored her instinctual drives, repressed the anger and hurt. What was wrong with her now? What had changed?

The door to the medical suite swung open.

Declan stood in the frame, those familiar blue eyes locking on her as he placed his hand over the new hole in his T-shirt, and everything went quiet.

The tension in her chest eased, and she stood a bit straighter. Right. Declan Monroe hadn't died after all. He'd cheated death. Twice. She took a single step toward him, caught in the gravitational pull she'd never been able to resist.

"Don't take too long, Doc. Everyone's waiting for you." Anthony crossed the waiting area filled with comfortable chairs and an empty receptionist's desk to the large oak doors of the main conference room. Swinging them open, he didn't wait for her before heading inside.

Leaving her and Declan alone.

She tamped down the anxiety clawing up her throat. "How's your side—"

"This is where you work." The smile she'd dreamed of seeing again flashed wide, hiking her blood pressure higher. So easygoing but gut-wrenching at the same time. "Good as new," he said. "Thanks."

"Good." Nodding, Kate rolled her bottom lip into her mouth and bit down, a nervous habit she'd picked up to distract herself when reality crept in. Which happened all too often. She scratched at the back of her neck in another attempt to lock it out. What was she supposed to say to the man who'd supposedly died because she failed to recognize the warning signs in her own patient? "Tell me where the hell you've been. Because none of this makes sense."

The words slipped out. She clenched her fists to ease the stress that had been building since Elliot had given her the photo of Declan in downtown Anchorage a month ago.

The stubble along his jawline shifted as he ran his hand over his face. Closing the distance between them, he heightened her awareness of him with every step. "Not much to tell. I woke up in a hospital alone. I didn't know where I was or what had happened. Who I was. I could barely move because of the pain in my chest, and no matter how hard I tried... I couldn't remember anything."

She held her breath as he raised one hand toward her face. This wasn't real. Soon she'd wake up, realize she'd been living a beautiful nightmare, and the grief would crush her again. But then he touched her. Her eyes drifted closed as he framed her face, and she leaned into his warmth. Wrapping her hand around his, she forced herself to look at him. To learn his face all over again.

"I remembered you for the first time three weeks after I left the hospital, and I knew I had to find you." Declan brushed his thumb across her cheek. Too soon, he pulled away, taking his body heat with him, and the brightness in his gaze dimmed. "I remembered other things, too. Bits and pieces. But nothing that explained how I ended up shot."

"You don't remember anything before waking up in the hospital?" Her mouth dried. Retrograde amnesia. Partial or total loss of every memory he'd ever lived. She'd studied cases back in her doctoral program at University of Oregon, but never imagined she'd be involved in the real-life nightmare that came with the condition. But he hadn't sustained any head or brain injuries as far as she knew during the shooting. Which suggested trauma. His brain had blocked the incident as a way of protecting itself. "Your parents, your work, your favorite food?"

"Nothing. Guess that means I have a lot to catch up on." His attention drifted to the top of her shirt collar, to the largest of her scars. Declan's voice turned to gravel. "Your scar looks like mine. How many bullets did they pull from you?"

She gave in to the urge to cover up, rubbing the fabric of her shirt collar between her fingers. They were a reminder of the worst night of her life, the onset of a lifetime of pain and grief, a kind of death sentence that she'd go through the rest of her life alone.

But he wasn't dead. He was here.

His condition might let up. She'd have to dig into her research, call a former colleague to be sure, but he might remember the life they had together, the years they'd spent together. Hope spread hard and fast, and Kate gave in for just a moment. To remember what it felt like.

Bullets. He'd asked about bullets. "Three."

"They catch the bastard who did it? Your patient." The blue in his eyes turned to ice, the tendons between his neck and shoulder visibly tightening. Her insides went cold, her instincts on alert. The man she'd married—the one she'd built an entire life with—had never shown signs of aggression in front of her, despite it being a large part of his job inside the FBI's serial crime unit. So who exactly had come back from the dead? Her husband or somebody else entirely?

"My teammate, Elliot, found him a few weeks after I started working for Blackhawk Security. Nearly six months after the shooting. He's one of those people who likes to know everything there is to know about the people he works with, and I wasn't an exception."

She slipped her hands into her cargo jacket—no, *his* jacket—pockets, but the guilt she'd shouldered only weighed heavier in her stomach. She'd done this to him—to them. She'd been so blinded by her own personal life, she hadn't seen what was happening right in front of her. How many other patients had she failed? How many lives had been changed due to her negligence?

"Brian Michaels had been off his medication for a few months. Toxicology screen came back for additional medication I wasn't aware he'd been taking. The steroids only increased his aggressive behavior to the point..." She didn't need to tell Declan the results. He'd lived them, same as her. "He's in a psychiatric ward here in the city. Sentenced to twenty years for murder."

"If he's locked up, then who do I have to thank for a bullet in my side tonight?" Declan asked.

"I don't know." Kate turned toward the conference room door and the entire Blackhawk Security team waiting for her briefing. She'd almost lost him—again—but this time would be different. Wrenching the large oak door open, she leveled her chin, more determined than she'd been in months. Whatever didn't kill her this time had better run. "Let's find out."

"Looks like we've got a new case." A heavily muscled man seated at the head of the table stood. "Sullivan Bishop. I run the place." He closed in on them, hand extended.

Shaking his hand, Declan noticed the guy moved with measured strength, and if Declan had to guess, the founder of Blackhawk Security was former military. The dirt under Sullivan's nails said this definitely wasn't a man who sat behind the desk while his team ran cases he wasn't willing to get his hands dirty with first.

"You've already met Anthony." Sullivan acknowledged the silent and armed weapons expert standing against one wall. "Elizabeth Dawson is our network security analyst."

A dark-haired woman with a heart-shaped face and leather jacket nodded.

"Vincent Kalani runs forensics." Pointing to the massive wall of muscle on the other side of Kate, Sullivan took his seat. Long black hair brushed across the guy's shoulders, an overgrown beard hiding his expression. "And Elliot Dunham here is the one who discovered you're still alive."

"Welcome back to the land of the living." Elliot extended two fingers in a wave, one foot stacked over the opposite knee. Storm-gray eyes zeroed in on Declan, making the hairs on the back of his neck stand on end. The guy was studying him. Every move. Every word out of his mouth. Looking for secrets? Something to use? Declan checked his expression. Not happening.

"Kate's already given us a briefing on your death," Sullivan said. "Why don't you fill us in on the rest, so we can find the bastard who took a shot at my profiler tonight, Mr. Monroe?"

Declan took a seat at the large conference table with one hand positioned over the bullet hole in his side. A vast view of the Chugach mountain range was visible through the span of windows behind Sullivan Bishop. Funny how Declan could name each peak along the range but couldn't remember his own damn name, where he'd worked before waking up in the hospital or the fact he'd been married. His senses automatically settled on the woman sitting beside him. His wife. Hell, were they even still married since he'd been declared dead?

He studied the rest of the team, the weight of their attention settling on him. "What do you want to know?"

"Where'd you go after you left Providence Alaska Medical Center?" Elizabeth leaned forward in her chair, her chocolate-brown gaze flickering to Kate for a moment before she refocused on him. The laptop in front of her highlighted the dark circles beneath her eyes, the softness around her middle exaggerated by a too-large maternity shirt. New mother.

"Brother Francis Shelter." He pressed his back into his chair, stretching the brand-new stitches in his side, and braced against the table. "It's not much, but I get a hot meal every night, a place to sleep, and they don't ask questions I can't answer."

There was a soft gasp from Kate as she massaged the thin skin of her left temple.

"Anyone ever follow you, or you get the feeling you were being watched?" This one from the one Sullivan had called Vincent. Based on his line of questioning, Declan pegged him as former law enforcement. A cop? Federal agent? The tattoos climbing up the guy's neck had already started showing their age. All done at the same time. Declan guessed four, five years max, but Blackhawk was fairly new, and no cop would be able to get away with ink like that unless it'd been part of a cover identity. Undercover work then.

About two months after regaining consciousness, Declan had started picking up on those kinds of details. Small things at first. The small amount of mud on the shoes of one of the shelter's other residents. The way the same man had disappeared when Anchorage PD had cleared out Buffer Park for the night. Almost as if Declan had been drawn to the guy's activities. But there'd never been a point where he'd picked up on being watched. Nobody had followed him to that house tonight, either. He was sure of it. "No. Never."

"What about your consulting case, Kate?" Sullivan landed an assessing gaze on his profiler, fingers tapping on the gleaming surface of the table. "Or any of your other cases where someone might've left unhappy?"

"Anchorage PD and the FBI only brought me in this morning to run a profile for a serial murder case. There hasn't been time for me to make any conclusions or to connect me with the investigation." There was little inflection in Kate's voice, as though she were a woman dictating her grocery list into her phone instead of a woman who'd nearly been shot a couple hours ago. Shifting in her seat, she cast her gaze to the paperwork set before her. "Given the fact I resemble all three of the case's victims, a connection isn't impossible, but the killer's MO includes an arrow and crossbow. No guns."

Every cell in Declan's body caught fire. She was the possible target of a serial killer? He set his teeth against the rising flood of possession. This was her job, and from what he'd gathered from her notes back at the house, she was damn good at it. Despite the fact they'd been married, he was sitting next to a stranger thanks to some dramatic event he couldn't remember. He had no claim on her safety, but he would find the bastard who'd tried to hurt her. With or without Blackhawk Security's help.

"Is Michaels still behind bars?" Sullivan asked. "He's already proven this kind of thing is right up his alley."

"Yes, as far as I know." Kate's hand constricted around the arm of her chair, her knuckles white against the coffee-colored leather.

"Liz, let's follow up with Corrections," Sullivan said. "Michaels has family, friends. One of them might not have been too happy about the way his case was handled."

"On it." Elizabeth made a note on the small notepad beside her. "Shouldn't take too long."

An automatic response had Declan interlacing his fingers between Kate's. Some part of him deep down considered her well-being more important than his own. Or was his body's response an attempt to recover even just a sliver of the memories he'd lost by physically connecting with the one person it recognized the most? A war had already erupted inside of him. Between his irrational urge to protect the wife he'd left behind, the compulsion to make her shooter pay and the need to uncover his past, Declan had to make a choice. "What about me? Could there be a threat from the time before I woke up in the hospital? Something to do with my job or family member?

Kate pulled her hand back, setting it in her lap.

Surprise infiltrated through the wall of certainty he'd built.

"Now there's where things get interesting," Elliot said. "I mean, aside from the fact your surgeon apparently tried to pass off a body in the hospital morgue as you to avoid having to answer for his patient suddenly missing from his hospital bed." He slid a file folder across the table. "Which I have him admitting to on audio, by the way. That guy isn't going to be cutting anyone open anytime soon."

Declan caught the folder before it dove off the edge, his name clearly on the tab's label. He'd run from the hospital so fast, he hadn't thought to read the patient chart in his room. For the past year, he'd assumed a different name, guessed at his age and birth date and had been searching records every week for a lead. His first instinct had been to run. He didn't know why. Only remembered the need to get as far from the hospital as possible. But this file… He had the answers he'd been looking for right in his hand.

Flipping open the cover, he skimmed the first page. "I worked with the FBI's Behavioral Analysis Unit for eight years. In their serial crime division. Special Agent Declan Monroe." A copy of his federal ID was right there in full color.

He studied Kate's expression, but she'd shut him out, intent on the design etched into the massive conference table. A profiler and a special agent who hunted criminals. Was it their work that had brought them together in the first place?

He scanned the list of his recent cases, but nothing stood out or jump-started another memory. "I don't recognize any of these old cases."

"But the perps might recognize you," Sullivan said. "Liz, get an update on Special Agent Monroe's past cases with the FBI, too. See if one of the suspects has been holding on to a grudge, and we'll work from there. The sooner the better."

"You got it." Elizabeth nodded, then stood, taking her laptop with her.

She wouldn't be the only one going through those cases. Declan's grip tightened on the stack of papers inside his file. Elliot had dug up the past, but this was Declan's job. *His* marriage. *His* life. He'd do whatever it took to get it back.

"Vincent, go back to Kate's house and dig as many bullets out of those walls as it takes to see if we can get a print, a ballistics match or anything to identify the shooter." Sullivan rounded the table as the forensics expert stood and followed Elizabeth out the door. "Anthony, tag along with Vincent in case the shooter gets an itch to finish the job. Elliot, you're on Kate's cases. I want to know if any of our current or past clients have had a problem with her since she came back from leave."

Came back from leave? Confusion rippled through Declan, which was common these days. He hauled himself to his feet as the meeting had obviously concluded. There had to be someone—other agents he'd worked with, a boss, a partner—who'd help him get his hands on his old case files.

"I admire you, Kate." Elliot straightened, nodding with a closemouthed smile. He rolled back his shoulder as though his muscles had stiffened up. "Took you two full weeks to get someone to start shooting at you. That's longer than I've gone."

"Thanks, Elliot. My client files are in my office." Kate stood, expression guarded. She pushed her chair back into the table without a single glance in Declan's direction. She nodded. "I need to start my profile on the FBI's serial case and check in with Special Agent Dominic."

Declan scrubbed his hand down his face. Name didn't ring a bell. Although, if Special Agent Dominic was working out of the Anchorage field office, he might've been one of Declan's peers before he "died." Dominic could have information relevant to tonight's shooting.

The oak doors swung open, and Elizabeth was there with her laptop balanced on her forearm. Chocolate-brown eyes wide, she shifted her attention from Declan to Kate, then onto her boss. "You wanted me to see if a family member or friend of Michaels might be holding a grudge. Well, I didn't get that far."

The network security analyst turned her laptop toward them, the photo of an older man, Caucasian with graying hair and puffy cheeks, on the screen. "Michaels was released from Holding three weeks ago due to overcrowding."

Chapter Three

Aware of the sweat that had broken out along her spine, Kate tried to swallow the sour taste of fear. She gripped the edge of her desk as hard as she could, supplying physical input to her muscles in an attempt to wrap her head around the news.

She'd taken refuge in her office. A few minutes to herself, that was all she needed, to get back the small bit of control she'd held on to these last couple weeks. She shook her head with a burst of disbelief. Control. Just a figment of her imagination.

Brian Michaels, her former patient who'd grown obsessed with having her for himself, had been released from prison. It wasn't supposed to be this way. He'd taken everything from her, and he was supposed to suffer for it.

"Michaels is never going to hurt you again, Kate." Declan slipped into her peripheral vision without warning. Soundless. He the predator, her the prey. The single lesson that'd been hammered into her brain over and over throughout her profiling years: behavior reflected personality. Declan's new behavior—the aggressive, sarcastic, seemingly unfazed kind—reflected a far different personality than the one she'd known.

His tone dipped into dangerous territory, raising the hairs on the back of her neck. "Or he'll die trying."

Overlaying her fear was a deep, deep anger. Anger at Michaels. For his release. For the shooter who'd put a bullet in Declan's side tonight. For the fact that no matter how hard she'd tried to blind herself from the truth the last few hours, the nagging feeling in her gut wouldn't disappear.

Kate raised her gaze to his, the bones in her fingers screaming for release. The man standing in front of her wasn't her husband. Same features, same body, same color hair. But the hardness in those brilliant blue eyes when he looked at her revealed Declan—*her* Declan—had died that night a year ago.

She forced her fingers to release the desk. "What's your name?"

"The federal ID in my file says Declan Monroe." That damn smile attempted to cool the burn blazing through her as he shoved his hands into his jeans pockets. "But I have the feeling you already knew that."

A humorless laugh escaped her throat as she closed Michaels's file and pushed it to the side of her desk. She wouldn't show weakness. Not now. Not ever. As far as anyone knew, she was emotionless, and she'd keep it that way. It'd been the most effective buffer for pain thus far. "I meant the name you've been using. What do you want me to call you?"

"I adopted a name after I left the hospital." His expression softened. "But Declan is fine. That's who I am, right? Gotta get used to it."

"Right." She nodded. Reaching across the desk, she gathered her client files to hand over to Elliot. Investigating her clients wouldn't do Blackhawk's private investigator any good. With Michaels's release, Kate had a pretty good idea where to look to find the shooter. After all, it was like Sullivan had said in the conference room: Michaels, who'd turned her life upside down once, had already shown a preference for guns.

She would help her team and Anchorage PD find the shooter. Then she'd get Declan the help he needed to move on with his life. Without her.

"I've already done the background check on Michaels," she said. "His sister is the only family he has left. He's probably hiding out at her property."

"Kate." Declan set his hand on top of hers holding the file, and an unfamiliar electric surge bolted up her arm.

Kate pushed away from the desk, knocking into her chair as oxygen left her lungs. The chair's wheels protested against the hard plastic beneath it, and she shot one hand behind her to catch herself from hitting the floor. Her throat swelled in an instant as she struggled to keep her balance. "Don't."

She forced herself to take a deep, calming breath. "Please, don't."

"I'm sorry." Palms raised in surrender, he backed away from the desk. "I didn't mean to hurt you—"

"You didn't." She struggled to keep her expression neutral. She'd overreacted, but just as she'd discovered in the conference room when he'd reached for her hand, when he touched her, she hurt.

More than the bullet wounds. More than the grief burrowing a hole through her entire being. She'd prayed for nothing over the last year but to have her husband back, but the reality of it was he hadn't come back. He might be standing in front of her, but he didn't know her, didn't remember their marriage, didn't know the green cargo jacket she wore every day actually belonged to him. Or that she'd finally had the guts to take off her wedding ring when she came back to work two weeks ago. Giving in to those innocent touches, of letting hope that he'd remember everything between them drown out the pain, was a risk she wasn't willing to take.

Swiping a stray hair out of her face, she collected Michaels's file once again. She cleared her throat. "The shelter probably isn't safe anymore. Is there anywhere else you can go tonight?"

"I'm not leaving you." Declan came around the desk. His hand rose, but he didn't touch her. He was too close, but she fought the urge to pull away again. To prove he didn't affect her—nothing did. "Tell me what the hell just happened."

She was suddenly far too aware of his proximity,

and her breath came a bit faster. His clean, masculine scent worked deep in her lungs, and her stomach twisted.

She gave in to her instinctual urge and tugged away, needing space between them. A lot of it. She lifted her chin. No point in keeping the truth from him. Didn't matter if he was the man she'd married or not. They'd be working this investigation together. "You're not him."

Saying the words made them real, made the ache behind her rib cage hurt a bit more.

"Your husband." Declan backed off, taking his body heat with him. A coldness ran through her as he seemed to sink in on himself. He scrubbed a hand over his five o'clock shadow, the bristling loud in her ears. "And here I thought getting shot in the gut was the worst that could happen to me today. If I'm not him, then who am I?"

"No." She blinked to clear her head, palms pressed together in front of her as she closed the distance between them. "I mean, you *are* him. You have his eyes. You have the same scar on your hand he got falling off his bike when he was ten and the dimple on the right side of your mouth. But you're—"

"Different?" Declan studied her office, but she got the sense it was more out of distraction than pure curiosity over how she'd decorated the space. "I read that could happen. Personality changes. Guess I didn't think much of it since I can't remember who I was from before."

The realization sat in her stomach like a rock. The small bit of air she'd been holding on to burned as it escaped up her throat. How could she have been so careless? He'd been through hell, too, if not worse. At least she'd been able to hold on to the memories of him. He…he had nothing. She had to remember that. "I'm sorry. I didn't mean… None of this is your fault. I—"

Commotion—yelling—reached her ears from outside her office.

"Kate!" a male voice yelled.

Recognition flared.

"Ryan?" Kate walked out from behind her desk, fully aware of her arm brushing against Declan's as she passed and wrenched open the door. The weight of Declan's gaze settled between her shoulder blades as a wall of black and white filled her vision.

Due to his six-foot-four height, she craned her head back to look up at Special Agent Ryan Dominic. Studying the hallway past his mountainous shoulder, she spotted both Anthony and Vincent as well as Dominic's partner, Kenneth Winter, waiting for her to raise the alarm. "What are you doing here? I got pulled onto your case this morning. I haven't started—"

"You weren't answering your phone." Ryan stared down at her with the darkest eyes she'd ever seen. Brown, almost black, but it was the control he kept over his expression that struck fear into the hearts of the violent offenders he hunted for the Bureau's Behavior Analysis Unit. Absolutely deadly. Made him one of the best agents on the government's payroll with higher arrest rates than any other agent. That technique had given him a nickname nobody dared say to his face. He was a good agent. A good friend, one she'd relied on since that dreadful night. She'd lost her husband in the shooting. He'd lost his partner.

"I had to hear about the shooting at your house from Anchorage PD." Dominic set both hands on her shoulders. "I came as soon as I could to make sure you were still alive. Why didn't you call me?"

"Good to see you again, Kate." Special Agent Kenneth Winter, in all his uptight glory, nodded around his partner's shoulder. He had medium length brown hair, thick eyebrows and steely brown eyes close to Dominic's in color. She didn't know Kenneth as well as his partner, but if the rumors she'd heard were true, Ryan had himself a go-getter on his team. Desperate to prove himself and to climb the internal ladder, Kenneth lobbied for the most violent and taxing cases. Usually with success. "This seems personal. I'm going to find a vending machine until you get your stuff sorted out."

"Thanks, Kenneth. It's fine, guys. I can take it from here." She waved toward Anthony and Vincent to take the physical tension filling the room down a notch. Pulling Dominic into her office, she closed the door behind him. "I'm alive and the team is running down leads with Anchorage PD as we speak. You didn't have to—"

"You're going to want to back away, friend." Declan moved beside her. If he'd had fur, his hackles would be raised.

It seemed every muscle Dominic owned stiffened. His hands curled into fists at his side. The special agent took a single step forward as he studied his former partner. "I don't believe it."

Declan watched every move Dominic made, blue eyes creasing at the edges like the investigator she remembered hunched over the dining room table, working his way through his most recent case.

"Right. Declan, this is Special Agent Ryan Dominic of the FBI's Behavioral Analysis Unit." She set her hand on his shoulder, throttling the warmth settling deep into her bones from the contact. "Your former partner."

PARTNER? THE AGENT standing in front of him sure didn't feel like a partner.

Declan eyed the Glock Dominic kept in the shoulder holster beneath that perfectly pressed suit. He didn't have any idea how he knew the agent's choice of service weapon, but the information was there, in the back of his head. Dominic worked for the FBI. Given the file on Declan's life, it stood to reason they'd met, but Dominic's body language said it wasn't a friendly relationship. Let alone a partnership. "You know me?"

Confusion cracked that carefully controlled expression, and the stiffness between the agent's shoulders and neck disappeared. Dominic widened his stance, hands on his hips. Close enough if he had to reach for his weapon. He brushed his jacket out enough for Declan to get a peek at his service weapon. A Glock. "I sure as hell hope so. We were partners for six years. Is this a joke?"

"No," Kate said. Her light vanilla scent clung to him, to his clothes, his skin, threatened to drag him deeper into the past his brain had barred him from remembering. The burn of her hand on his arm grounded him, kept him in the moment, but then it was gone. Again. He didn't blame her. She'd made it clear before the FBI had walked through her door. He wasn't her husband. At least, not the one she'd been expecting to come walking back into her life from the grave. "Ryan, Declan doesn't remember anything before the shooting. The trauma erased his memories."

"What?" A disbelieving laugh broke through the special agent's control but was gone faster than it appeared. Dominic ran a hand down his face and the stubble along his squared jawline. A hint of Latino heritage gave him the dark hair and eyes, but Declan pegged the agent as local from his accent. "They said you were dead. The FBI buried you, and all this time you've, what, been walking around Anchorage without any idea of who you are? Whose body is in your grave?"

"We don't know. The surgeon obviously has some explaining to do, but that about sums it up, yeah." They were wasting time here. The shooter could've already started planning another attempt on Kate's life. Could already be on the way to Blackhawk Security. Although getting through the front doors might take a small army considering how many armed operatives and security measures Declan had noted coming in, but he wasn't willing to take the chance. Not with the only lead he had to restoring his memory.

"This is unbelievable," Dominic said. "What do you remember then?"

"Ryan, it's a long story, and I promise I will explain it all later." Kate swiped the file from the edge of her desk and handed it to Dominic. "Right now, we need to find Brian Michaels and interrogate him about the shooting tonight. If he's off his meds again, I don't want him hurting anyone else. Can you pull some strings? Help us out?"

Ryan. Not Special Agent Dominic. Kate and his former partner were familiar with each other. Explained why the agent had touched her as soon as she opened the door. Declan locked his jaw against the unfamiliar rush of jealousy ripping through his chest. Exactly how close had his wife and Dominic gotten when he died?

"Michaels is out? This day keeps getting better and better." Dominic flipped through the file. "All right, I'll help you track down your shooter, but in the meantime, I'm getting you into a safe house. From this moment on, you're officially in protective custody." That dark gaze flickered to Declan as Dominic handed the folder back to Kate. "If Michaels is responsible for the shooting tonight, there's a chance he'll keep trying until he gets what he wants. As far as we know, that's you, and I'm not going to let him shoot at you a third time."

"The FBI can't protect her." Declan closed the distance between him and Kate, a possessiveness bubbling beneath the surface. Kate had escaped a killer twice. The odds of her surviving another attempt, even while in FBI custody, went down with every second the bastard was out there. Serial offenders only got better at what they did. They learned from experience, and the shooter wouldn't stop unless he was caught or killed. "I can."

Dominic folded his arms, stance wide. "You can't be serious. You just said you can't remember anything—"

"I'm not going into hiding," Kate said, "and I'm not going into protective custody. I can protect myself, or have you both forgotten who I work for?" She tilted her chin higher, Michaels's file in her hand.

In that instant, Declan had no doubt the woman standing in front of him could give the shooter a run for his money. Not just physically but mentally, and for an instant, he sensed exactly why he'd married her in the first place. Profilers were known to put themselves inside the heads of the criminals they hunted, and that meant knowing how the suspect would think, act and what their next step would be before they made a conscious decision.

Dominic lowered his hands to his sides, took a step toward her. "Kate—"

"I'll have my profile on your serial case ready as soon as I can, Special Agent Dominic." She motioned him to the door. "Until then, thank you for helping find Michaels. I appreciate it."

Dominic's nut-brown eyes darted to Declan again. Dropping his voice, the special agent leaned closer to Kate, making Declan's blood boil. "You're making a mistake. Call me when you realize that."

Kate didn't respond as Dominic wrenched open the office door and disappeared down the hall. Tension visibly drained from her as she faced Declan, but the exhaustion etched into her features didn't lessen. "He's not going to look for Michaels," she said. "My case doesn't come with an honorary award like the Hunter's does if he solves it."

The Hunter. Was that the serial case the FBI had brought her in to profile? According to news reports, three women had disappeared over the last year, their bodies found in the middle of the woods around Anchorage with a single arrow shot to the heart. All blonde. All athletic and in great shape. Similar to the woman standing less than two feet from him. "You seem sure of that."

"There isn't enough room in Ryan's life for friends *and* his ego. He'll work the Hunter case and leave Blackhawk to find our shooter." She studied him. "You want to know how close we are. Your former partner and your wife."

Had she read his thoughts or was his face just that easy to read? "It crossed my mind."

"We're friends. Nothing more. He brought dinners after I was released from the hospital, helped me arrange your funeral so I didn't have to. Like I said, Ryan doesn't have room for real relationships. He uses people to get what he wants, which usually involves a case he's working," she said.

Declan didn't have any right to ask, but the words clawed up his throat anyway. "Has there been anyone else?"

Her bottom lip parted from the top. "Are you asking because you're worried it will affect our investigation into the shooter or because you were my husband in a former life?"

"I shouldn't have asked." Taking Michaels's file from her hand, he headed for the door.

"After you died, I used to talk to you. Like you were still around," she said.

Her voice slowed his escape, prickling goose bumps along his arms. The pain in his side evaporated as he slowly turned back to face her.

A humorless laugh bubbled past her lips. "It sounds insane. I buried you. I knew you weren't coming back, but a part of me still held on to hope. Still prayed day after day to some greater power that the shooting, losing you, had all been some sick nightmare I'd wake up from any moment. But the months went by—a year—and I never woke up."

Declan couldn't move, couldn't think. He worked to swallow the tightness in his throat, but the anguish in her expression held him frozen. If she'd sought comfort in another man's arms, he had no logical reason to give in to the unexplained jealousy simmering in his veins. He couldn't remember their marriage, had only glimpses of her in his memories. That wasn't why he'd come back into her life.

He took a step toward her. "Kate—"

"I took my wedding ring off two weeks ago, Declan. There hasn't been anyone else, but I moved on." She massaged the line of lightened skin around her ring finger as she stared down at her hand. Lifting her chin, she lowered her hands to her sides and locked out the emotion that'd been there a few moments ago. "We'll find Michaels or whoever took those shots at us tonight. I'll help you get your life back, but after that, I think it's best we go our separate ways."

An invisible fist clenched inside his gut. Get his life back. What the hell did that even mean? He'd spent the last year in a shelter, digging into as many records as he could find to uncover his past without any luck.

According to the few legal documents he'd read in Blackhawk Security's file on him—combined with the handful of memories his brain had decided to vomit at random intervals—his life was standing on the other side of that desk. Kate Monroe was the key to his past, the only person who knew him before he'd woken up in a hospital bed. His likes, dislikes, if his parents were still alive, if he had siblings, the sources of his scars, how he'd chosen a career hunting criminals, if he'd been a good man, a good husband. A father?

"I understand." A lie. He didn't. The few glimpses

of memory he'd had of her had seemed happy enough. Her smiling as he came home, the echo of her laughter as they made a batch of vanilla cupcakes together and the flour had gotten on her nose and cheeks.

All of those memories combined had given him a mere fraction of the emotion burning through him now. This woman had been ingrained so deep in his neural pathways, not even amnesia had been able to force him to forget her. There had to be a reason.

Declan took in the lack of photos on her desk and forced himself to nod. He'd sure as hell find out why. "Lead the way."

Chapter Four

Her hand hovered above the dead bolt to her apart-ment. She'd never brought anyone here. Not the team. Not anyone, but bringing Declan here seemed too…intimate. As though she were inviting him into her life. But he'd been a large part of her life, part of her, too.

Kate shoved the key into the lock and twisted. Automatically reaching for the light beside the door, she braced for his reaction.

Stark white walls and furniture, no personal ef-fects, packing boxes everywhere. It'd been nine months since she'd moved in, but the thought of making it permanent had almost been too much. The two-bedroom, two-bath high-rise apartment had gotten her as far across the city as she could get and still stay within range for the team if they needed her.

Beautiful mountain views commanded atten-tion through the wall of ceiling-to-floor windows. The sun had yet to come up, so only the twinkling lights of Anchorage were visible from here. But in a few hours, red, pinks and yellows would crest over the peaks and light up this entire room. She'd never missed a sunrise in this apartment, in love with the idea of starting a new day, a new life. Then again, sunrises were hard to miss when she spent most of the night awake anyway.

He couldn't go back to the shelter, and the thought of getting him a hotel room for the night while there was a shooter on the loose pooled dread at the base of her spine. At least here, she could protect him. Kate tossed her keys onto the small table near the door as Declan stepped inside.

Stress lines, deeper than she remembered, etched across his face. He'd spent the last year in a shelter. Hadn't really known much else since losing his memories. She couldn't imagine the thoughts running through his head right now. In the past three hours alone, he'd inexplicably been drawn to a house he'd never consciously stepped foot inside, gotten shot, discovered he'd been married and met a partner he hadn't known existed. The brain could only take so much before it cracked. She understood that from experience.

"I think I have a box of your old clothes in my bedroom closet," she said. "Feel free to clean up while I look for it, and then I can make us something to eat."

"That sounds great." He studied the space, nodding, then headed toward the hallway off to the left with a backpack in tow. "Thank you."

She heard the bathroom door close, but instead

of the stiffness draining from her neck and shoulders, Kate let herself slip down the wall and onto the floor.

For the first time since she'd seen him back in their old house, reality set in. Declan was here. Against all odds, he'd survived, and the breath rushed out of her.

The floor sucked at her, urging her to sink heavier into its supportive cradle, but the blood from Declan's wound had destroyed his clothes. Unless he felt comfortable walking around completely naked, she had to get up, had to find that last box full of his things she'd held on to.

Kate tapped the crown of her head against the door. "Can't stop now, Monroe."

The rain-like fall of shower water hitting tile grew louder down the hall as the bathroom door swung open. Pressure built in her chest as Declan appeared in nothing but a towel wrapped around his lean waist. Concern etched his expression as he caught sight of her on the floor, but she didn't have the strength to move. His dirty blond hair was thick and mussed as though he'd run his fingers through it. His mouth, full and sensual, pressed into a thin line. "Kate."

"I'm fine. I'm just…tired." The confession barely escaped her lips. These last few hours had ripped apart everything she'd worked for over the past year. She'd fought to control the anger pent up at having him taken away, she'd thrown herself into work in an attempt to distract herself, convinced herself she was finally moving on. She'd taken her wedding ring off before coming back to work for Blackhawk Security, but the truth was, she still kept it close.

Diving one hand into her jacket pocket, she showed him the thin gold band. She studied the inscription on the inside, their wedding date. "I thought taking this off would make it easier, but my finger feels naked without it. I feel unconnected." She closed her eyes. What she wouldn't give for a full night's sleep. "That doesn't even make any sense."

"It doesn't have to." Declan came toward her, his bare feet padding across the hardwood floor, and she couldn't help but admire the view. Wide, muscled shoulders, the ridges and valleys of his six-pack, the outline of powerful thighs through the towel.

Lowering to sit down beside her, he chased the cold from her bones as he brushed against her. "You don't have to control anything. Not with me. You've been through hell as much as I have. You want to yell, cry, punch me in the face, hate me for coming back into your life? Do it. Do whatever you have to to work through this. Suffering in silence will only tear you apart."

A small laugh burst from her chest. "Repressing things is one of my favorite hobbies."

When they were married, she'd kept it all bottled up. To the point she didn't know whether she truly was experiencing emotion or if she only thought she should. She still didn't know sometimes. Declan had dealt with so much pain, so much sorrow on the job hunting the monsters, she hadn't wanted to add to any of it. Their marriage had depended on it. She had to stay strong, be there for him when he'd needed it the most, but that left no one there for her.

"Not anymore." Declan raised his hand, fingers sliding through a strand of hair that had fallen loose from her bun. He studied her from forehead to chin.

What did he see? How empty she'd become since his death? How much she'd missed him? How it took every ounce of control she possessed not to compare the man in front of her with her husband? She gave in to the way his dimple only showed up when he smiled at her, the way the scar on the tip of his left middle finger glided across her jaw.

"I'm starting to see why you're the only one I remember," he said.

The flood of pain and repression broke through the dam she'd built over the past few months. Her control vanished as he leaned into her, setting his lips against hers.

Warmth snaked through her. Every cell in her body intensified in awareness as he framed her face between his large hands. Her heart was beating too fast, all the blood rushing to her head. His scent filled her system. Everything that had happened over the past year vanished as he deepened the kiss. The blood, the horror, the mystery behind the why. With him, right here in this moment, she let it go— all of it. And she'd never felt so free in her life.

A small moan escaped her mouth as he pulled

her close, close enough her body pressed against the hard, muscled heat of his chest.

Kate fisted one hand low in his hair as pure need clawed through her. It'd been too long since she'd let someone touch her, care for her, hold her…she'd forgotten what it felt like.

He gripped his hand higher up on her arm, and she flinched as pain zinged down to her fingers.

"What is it?" he asked.

She pulled back, pulling her arm free of his hold. Studying the small hole in the arm of her cargo jacket, Kate sat back on her rear end. She pulled her sleeve to center the hole and studied the light ring of blood.

A bullet hole?

She'd been running off pure adrenaline, trying to catch up with the new reality that had crashed through her world in the past few hours. She hadn't noticed the burn of a bullet graze across her arm. "I literally didn't know that was there until this moment."

"What?" Declan surged to his knees, concern clear in his voice. His hand wrapped around her arm, careful to avoid the wound as he studied it closer. Violence gleamed in the sea-blue depths of his eyes. "That SOB is going to pay. Here, take off your jacket. Let me see how bad it is."

Kate diverted her attention to the hardwood floor as his towel shifted, and she pressed herself flat against the wall. She'd seen her husband naked countless times, but this…this was different. "That's okay. I just realized how very naked you are."

Declan glanced down, righted the towel with a hint of pink climbing up his neck and into his face. Nice to know there were still some things that could get to him. "Right. Okay, first, clothes, then we'll have a look at that wound."

"I'm fine." She'd recovered from far worse injuries. A bullet graze was nothing compared to the three rounds she'd taken in the past. "Go. Finish your shower. Nothing I haven't handled before, remember? I can—"

"Let me." His fingers brushed over her arm, raising goose bumps even through the thick fabric of her jacket. "Please."

A tugging at the base of her spine had her nodding at his request. He looked at her as though he needed to do this for her, as though he needed to make up for something. Which didn't make sense. None of this—the shooting tonight, the amnesia, the fact she'd been grazed—was his fault. He was just as much a victim as she'd been.

Kate settled her hand in her lap. She hadn't been fully hit. The wound wasn't bleeding anymore. Shouldn't be too hard to apply some ointment and bandage the area. "Okay."

"Don't move. I'll be right back." Declan straightened, disappearing down the hallway. The bathroom door clicked once more, and the flood of heat he'd generated inside of her drained.

Shoving to her feet, she cringed against the now

constant pain burning down her arm and headed toward her office. Saved by a bullet. How original. What had she been thinking, kissing him? How had she given up control so easily? The stranger currently in her guest bathroom was not her husband.

Kate located the box she needed from her office and hauled it out to the front room. Tearing away tape and flimsy cardboard, she held her breath against the sight of her husband's old things, items he'd cherished for years. She pulled the University of Alaska T-shirt from the top, the worn feel of the fabric still smooth in her hands, and stilled.

Declan had looked at her, and everything she'd worked to build to protect herself vanished. There was so much more in that blue gaze than she remembered, a warmth that hadn't ever been there before—a hardness.

Kate swallowed. She was almost afraid to find out what that more could mean. She closed the box, clean shirt in hand…afraid to hope.

STRENGTH. DARKNESS. The woman was an enigma he hadn't been able to read since confronting her in that house, but for a brief moment, it had been right there in her eyes as she'd kissed him. Desire. Warmth. The need to be cared for. And hell if his body hadn't responded. It'd been one of the most intense experiences he'd remember for years to come. Something no way in hell he'd forget.

For those fifteen seconds, Kate Monroe had let her guard down.

But even with that physical anchor to his past, nothing about her or that kiss had given him more information on the man he'd been before. Documents could only get him so far. His memories. They were all that mattered.

Declan toweled off, careful of the bullet wound, and dressed quickly, leaving his bloodied shirt in the small garbage can beside the pedestal sink. He'd taken wipe showers, eaten nothing but soup, slept on an uncomfortable cot after escaping from the hospital. But here, here in her too-white apartment, with her too-modern furniture and white tile, he felt more at home than he had anywhere else.

Because of her. What that meant, he had no idea.

Stepping out of the bathroom door, Declan's gut growled. When was the last time he'd eaten? Twenty-four hours? More? He couldn't remember the last thing he'd put in his mouth. Didn't matter; he didn't care if she planned on microwaving a frozen dinner. Whatever she'd started cooking had his full attention. Until he set sights on her.

Standing in front of the stove, she struggled to tape a bandage over the bullet graze on her arm. Kate bit down on the roll of tape to secure the adhesive over the graze but dropped the entire thing into a pot of boiling water in front of her. "That's not good."

"Should give it a nice, glue-like flavor, don't you think?" Declan rounded the granite-top island, taking in the shrimp, mushrooms, herbs, cream cheese and garlic already prepared and waiting on its gleaming surface. She'd cooked for him. Or…had tried to cook for him.

Gripping the tongs beside the stove, he dove in for the roll of tape, extracted it from a mess of pasta and set it on the counter. "Trust me, I won't be able to tell the difference."

Her laugh reverberated through him, and he followed the hint of pink into her cheeks.

Studying her injury, she placed a hand over the graze and stepped back. "You'd think after making this dish so many times, I'd get it right someday."

"Give me your arm." He reached for her hand, smooth skin gliding over the calluses in the center of his palm. Heat lanced through him, straight down his spine at the contact. Touching her—kissing her—might not have brought back any past memories, but he sure as hell didn't regret it. He just had to be careful from here on out.

He cleared his throat around the sudden swelling constricting his airway. "You cook a lot?"

"I think my pasta boiling skills already answered that for you." The weight of her attention bore into him as he worked to save the roll of partially melted medical tape. "I mostly live off the protein bars Sullivan provides for the office, but after the day you've had, I thought you might like something comforting. Cream cheese and carbs always hit the spot for me."

"Can't argue with that." He placed the gauze over her arm and ripped a piece of adhesive from the roll with his teeth. Securing the bandage in place, he tossed the first-aid supplies back into the open kit he hadn't noticed spread on the counter until now.

First getting him to the doctor, then offering her home to clean up in, and now she was making him dinner. What was it about this woman? Aside from the fact she hadn't just crossed his mind over the past year, she'd practically set up a permanent residence, he had no reason to trust her. Yet every time he thought of getting what he needed from her and leaving, of finding that shooter on his own, his gut clenched. "You're officially patched up."

"Thank you," she said.

"No problem." He cataloged the rest of the ingredients across the counter and rubbed his palms together. "I'm not sure how good I'll be, but I'm happy to help with whatever it is you have going on here. It's the least I could do since, you know, you saved my life."

"You'll have to put a shirt on." Jerking her chin toward the living room, she pointed out a gray T-shirt draped over one of the chairs. Her smile increased his blood pressure. She rubbed her hand over the bullet's graze in her arm, then motioned to his bare chest. "No telling what other kinds of accidents are going to happen while I attempt to cook. Wouldn't want all those pretty muscles to get burned in the process."

"Probably a good idea." He closed in on the T-shirt she'd laid out, rubbing the material between his fingers. University of Alaska. It was a men's shirt, and she'd said something about pulling a box of his old things before he'd taken a shower. Stood to reason that the shirt belonged to him.

Pulling the material over his head, he flinched against the sting of his stitches. "What can I do to help?"

"You can mince garlic while I clean the shrimp." Kate grabbed a clean cutting board and a knife, setting them beside her station on the counter. Her deep purple nail polish caught the gleam of lights from overhead as she moved between ingredients, and it somehow represented everything he'd imagined her to be. Intriguing, sexy, independent.

Maneuvering to her side, he breathed her vanilla scent in a bit deeper, let it fill him with a renewed sense of appreciation. After everything this woman had been through—the shooting, the surprise of his resurrection, the exhaustion—she'd put his needs ahead of her own. Hell, if that didn't earn his respect. A woman like that was a rare creature, one that needed to be protected. She cared, she sacrificed, she pushed through.

He was the only one standing between her and another attempt on her life. He'd be damned if he failed her again.

"Why the change to profiling?" he asked.

"What?" Her hold on one shrimp faltered, and it fell onto the counter.

"You said Brian Michaels was your patient, but you're profiling for Blackhawk and the FBI now. Why the change?" Declan reached for another clove of garlic, brushing the edge of his hand against hers.

Awareness shot straight up his arm, of her shallow breathing, the way her beautiful green eyes widened slightly, the tightening of her fingers around the handle of the knife. Something inside him responded to her on a deep, instinctual level. It was probably due to the fact they'd been married, been intimate, that his brain refused to forget her even after the most dramatic event of his life. For all he knew, the hitch in his breathing and heart rate had more to do with muscle memory than any real connection between them. Because she'd made it perfectly clear: he wasn't her husband anymore.

He positioned the flat edge of his knife over the garlic and slammed his hand on top. Maybe a bit too hard. "Can't imagine putting yourself in the head of a killer like the Hunter does miracles for your outlook on life."

"Oh." Kate stared at the shrimp in her hand, rolling her bottom lip into her mouth. The tendons between her neck and shoulders strained. She swiped the back of one hand across her forehead, then shifted her weight onto her other foot. Obvious anxiety deepened the small indents between her eyebrows. She didn't want to talk about it.

"Hey, I'm sorry." He forgot the garlic, turning into her. He smothered the urge to touch her again. The intense reaction that sparked every time he laid a hand on her wouldn't do either of them a damn bit of good right now. "You don't have to tell me anything. We just met. We don't know each other well enough—"

"No, it's okay." But she still wouldn't look at him. The slight tremor in her hand settled as she set down the paring knife she'd been using on the shrimp. "As a psychologist, I encouraged my patients to talk in order to work through their issues. You'd think it'd be easy for me to follow my own advice."

Only the sound of the boiling water behind them on the stove drowned the hard pounding of his heartbeat behind his ears.

"I let my personal life get in the way of helping my patient." She busied herself by ripping a tail off the last shrimp and tossed it into the ceramic bowl with the rest. "Michaels was spiraling out of control, and I didn't have any clue. I missed the signs. I didn't know he'd stopped taking his medications."

Kate raised her green gaze to his, gripping the edge of the granite countertop. "When Sullivan approached me to work for the team, to help catch the bad guys and get justice for those who the police couldn't or wouldn't help, I said yes."

Everything inside of him went cold. He'd gotten a hint of her guilt back at the house, with her hands working to stop the blood flow from his wound. But this...

Declan closed the short space between them, unable to keep his distance any longer. Sliding his hand across the back of hers, he peeled her white-knuckled grip from the countertop and massaged his thumbs into her palm. "You don't have to carry that guilt, Kate. Michaels knew what he was doing. He would've found a way—"

"You don't understand. I didn't only lose you that night, Declan." Kate pulled her hand from his, tugging up the bottom hem of her T-shirt. Smooth, creamy skin slid beneath his fingers as he gave in to the urge to see if she was as soft as she looked. But his gaze homed in on the lump of scar tissue an inch or so under her belly button, dead center. White, puckered and angry, an exact match for the four scars he carried. "I lost our baby, too, and I'm not going to let Michaels get away with it."

Chapter Five

"You were…pregnant?" Light blue eyes slowly raised to hers. "With our baby."

"I carry a lot of guilt for what happened that night, but it only plays a small part compared to the anger." Kate lowered her shirt, turned to the pasta boiling over on the stove and flipped off the burner. She blinked back the burn of tears. She didn't cry. She didn't feel. She didn't let her guard down. She had control, and she wasn't about to break down for the millionth time in front of a complete stranger.

Except when Declan threaded his hand around her waist, pulled her into him and held her, that control shattered. In a matter of seconds, aching sobs ripped through her, but he only held her tighter, grounding her.

"We're going to find Michaels," he said. "Together. And we're going to make sure he gets everything that's coming to him."

She didn't know how long they stood there, the pasta overcooking, the scent of garlic thick on the air. She didn't care. For a split second, she wasn't alone. She wasn't standing on her own. He held her up, gave her the strength. He took that pain away.

Kate rested her head on his shoulder, her nose pressed into the column of his throat as her palm found his heart. She counted off the beats as the strong, steady drum hammered through her. For the first time since the shooting, right here, right now, safety was within reach. Which didn't make sense. She'd just met him, really, but something deep down—something she'd buried in that coffin—said he wouldn't hurt her.

"You can forgive yourself right now, angel. Michaels was in charge of his actions. Not you," he said. "That guilt is only going to destroy you."

Her breath hitched. Impossible. Kate swiped at her face and put a few inches of space between them, her fingers skimming down his arm. "What did you call me?"

He narrowed his eyes on her. "Angel."

"Why?" Desperation clawed through her as she fisted her hands in his shirt, the one he used to wear on the weekends, used to wear to bed. The one she'd recently packed away because she couldn't stand the thought of getting rid of it. "Why that name? Why angel?"

"Your blond hair, your perpetuity for putting everyone else first before yourself." Declan ran a hand through his already mussed hair. "I guess it kind of slipped out. If you're offended—"

"No. I'm not offended." She forced her fingers to release him and smoothed the creases her damp palms had pressed into the shirt. It was a coincidence. Nothing more. Nothing she should sink her nails into. Her pulse slowed as she breathed him in. Slow, deep breaths. The dam had been broken when he'd kissed her, when he'd coaxed her to relive the pain she'd suppressed for so long. She was out of control. She had to get a hold on reality. "You...you used to call me that. Before."

Once upon a time, she'd been his angel. But now...

"I'm sorry, Kate. I didn't know." He stepped into her, hands out, but every muscle in her body tightened in response.

Declan backed down, put space between them at her reaction. "It slipped out, but I'll be careful in the future. I won't call you that again."

Kate forced herself to take a deep breath. Then another. "No. It's not your fault. It's been a crazy day. Emotions are running high. I'm... I'm really tired, and it looks like dinner is ruined anyway."

She maneuvered around him, pointing down the hall toward her bedroom. Distance. She needed distance. The past eight hours had ripped her apart, but even with his attempt to piece her back together, the human body and mind could only take so much.

"I think it's best we get some rest before looking for Michaels, but you're welcome to raid the fridge and the pantry if you're hungry. Please, take whatever you need, and there's extra bedding in the linen closet."

The apartment blurred in her vision as she escaped down the hall, her chest too tight, her head spinning. She forced herself to close the door behind her softly, then collapsed against it. She didn't have the strength for this. For years, she'd helped her patients become stronger, better versions of themselves, helped them work through their trauma. Kate rubbed the base of her palms into her eye sockets. Why then couldn't she help herself?

She shoved to her feet. She needed to shower, drink a glass of water, get something to eat. There were people out there who needed her help, and she wouldn't be doing her team or the FBI any good in this condition.

Heading for the bathroom, she stripped out of her bloodstained clothing, then twisted the shower knob to hot. Steam filled the bathroom quickly, and she breathed a bit easier.

Declan hadn't done anything wrong. None of this was his fault. She needed to apologize to him, explain. They'd be working this case together. Despite her internal battle, he was as much a part of this as she was.

In minutes, she toweled off and dressed in her favorite pair of sweats and oversize T-shirt. As she reached for the bedroom door, three knocks reverberated through her.

"Kate?" Declan's voice was a soothing remedy to the panic consuming her vision, and it took a moment to center herself. Of course, he'd come to check on her. From the moment he planted himself in that bullet's path to save her life, he'd proven that part of her husband had survived the trauma. "You okay?"

Hand on the doorknob, she put the armor he'd stripped back into place. The man on the other side of the door wasn't her husband—never would be—and she had to accept that reality. They'd have to work together to find and question Michaels, she'd help him get his life established, get him out of that shelter, but that was as far as it would ever go between them.

Kate swung the door inward, faced with the sight of shrimp linguine in creamy mushroom sauce. Her mouth parted as her stomach gargled with hunger pains at the aroma. "You finished cooking it."

"Didn't want our hard work go to waste." Declan offered her the plate, complete with a fork and a glass of white wine, the muscles down his arms bunching as he moved. That gut-wrenching smile did its job as his fingers made contact with hers. What was it about touching him that had her all twisted in knots?

"Thank you." Heat penetrated through the plate into her hand, but the sensation exploding from her chest demanded her attention. Nobody had ever cooked for her before. Her own grandparents who'd raised her had worked full-time and hadn't had the time or the energy to do much else but provide packets of ramen noodles for Kate and her younger brother. But this…this wasn't ramen.

"Least I could do for you giving me a place to crash tonight." Declan nodded and turned to head back toward the living room, but Kate took a step after him, her heart in her throat.

"You don't have to eat alone." That sensation behind her sternum rocketed through the rest of her body as he slowed to a stop in the hallway. Ridges and valleys of muscle flexed along his back, then he faced her, blue eyes assessing every change in her expression. Looking for another crack in her armor? He wouldn't find it.

"I don't want to complicate things between us more than they already are, Kate." Rolling his fingers into fists at his side, standing there as though he were ready for battle, he looked exactly like the special agent she'd known him to be. Would she ever be able to separate the two in her mind? He closed the distance between them, one step at a time. "I don't intend to start anything I can't finish."

The tendons behind her knees weakened. Air rushed from her lungs. What did that mean?

"I'll give you one more chance to decide and be sure this time." His voice graveled, raising the hairs on the back of her neck.

Her hold on the plate faltered as his exhale grazed the oversensitive skin across her collarbone. Why did it feel as though she wasn't asking him to eat dinner with her but something far more dangerous? Far more tempting?

"Ask me again," he said.

Kate rolled back her shoulders, leveled her chin. He'd saved her life back at the house, cooked her dinner, and she was an adult. She could take care of herself, protect herself. And maybe the thought of eating the pasta alone hollowed her insides a bit more now that their fates had intertwined again.

She'd been alone for so long. Kind of felt nice to have someone else to talk to outside of work.

"All right. Have dinner with me," she said.

His expression softened with a one-sided smile. Declan took the glass of wine from her, then threaded his free hand around hers. Instant warmth shot straight into her bones and counteracted the pain in her arm from the fresh wound. But this time, she didn't flinch away.

He pulled her into the kitchen, set her glass on the countertop and slid one of the two bar stools out for her. All of the mess from food preparations had been taken care of, the island cleaned.

"You didn't have to do any of this." Kate took a seat on the bar stool, surprised to already find silverware laid out. As though he'd expected her all along.

When had she become so predictable? Or was it the fact he seemed to read her better than anyone else ever had? Wasn't necessarily a bad thing. They were going to be partners for the foreseeable future. Because as much as she hated to admit it openly, she had the feeling Michaels wasn't going to be found unless he wanted to be.

"No trouble at all, but for the record, you did most of the heavy lifting. The thought of deveining those shrimp makes me gag." His deep laugh did funny things to her insides as Declan took a seat beside her, his body heat sliding up her arm. He lifted his own glass of wine, clinking it against hers. "To partners."

She wrapped her fingers around the clear crystal, the weight of his gaze on her the entire time. The decision had already been made. Her purpose— to bring the man who'd shot at them tonight to justice—would be greater than her pain.

Kate clinked her glass against his and took a heavy sip. "To partners."

SHE WAS ASLEEP in her bed—alone—her breathing heavy and slow.

Declan skimmed his fingers down the door frame to her bedroom and shut the door behind him quietly before heading back to the living room. She'd fallen asleep on the couch as they'd watched some mindless television show, and he hadn't been able to resist tucking her in for the night.

She'd been pregnant. With his baby.

Rubbing his palms down his face, he collapsed onto one of the too-white sofas. What the hell was he supposed to do with that information?

He shouldn't have pushed her for an answer. Should've minded his own damn business. Because the last thing he ever wanted was to see that woman cry again. Angels weren't supposed to cry, yet every crack in her expression had gutted him from the inside. And he'd do anything he had to to ensure nobody hurt her. Himself included.

"She doesn't deserve what you're going to do to

her." He'd only brought pain and suffering into her life. Staying longer would only destroy her more.

Alone, in the dark, he took in the magical expanse of the city through the floor-to-ceiling windows. Kate had an entire team to track down the bastard who'd taken a shot at her tonight. She didn't need him. He wasn't an investigator anymore and she had everything and everyone she needed to get the job done. All he'd managed to do was mess with her head. And that kiss… He was selfish for using her to prompt another set of memories.

But she was the only tie to the past he had, the only one who could give him his life back.

The tablet Sullivan Bishop had loaned him for the investigation brightened across the room with a silent notification, reflecting off the wall of glass in front of him. Shoving away from the couch, Declan crossed the room and unplugged it from the charger. An email forwarded by Blackhawk's network security analyst to the in-box she'd set up for him and Kate's company email. Could have something to do with their case.

He pressed his thumb to the home button.

The screen flashed white, taking him directly to the original email. From Special Agent Dominic. The attachments laid out all the evidence, the witness statements, crime scene analysis, everything the FBI had on the serial killer Kate had been asked to profile, the Hunter.

Declan found himself tapping on each attachment, skimming over the details of all three victims and the scenes where they'd been left.

Dense trees, thick dried grass, out in the middle of the woods. Off the trail so as not to be found easily. Only the killer knew how many more were out there, waiting to be recovered. No meaningful connection between the victims as far as the FBI had been able to tell. They varied in age, height, weight. Nothing similar but their appearance. Short blond hair, athletic, green eyes. His heart raced, and he swiped through the rest of the attachments to clear his head of the look in their eyes as they stared up into the sky. All three women looked like Kate.

Declan sat in a nearby chair. Anchorage was as diverse a city as it could get. What were the odds the Hunter lured three Caucasian women to their deaths from the same location? Unless—

"You know, a normal person wouldn't stay up late to review photos of bodies." Her voice penetrated through the thick haze the puzzle had built.

He closed his eyes against a surge of regret. Hell, he hadn't heard her approach, too embedded in the case. He got like that sometimes—invested—but now he understood why. He'd worked for the FBI. He'd hunted monsters. Standing, Declan faced her, his blood pressure spiking at the play of moonlight across her features. "I didn't mean—"

"Yes, you did. You were one of the best investigators the FBI has ever seen. I can understand the draw to solve one of their highest-profile cases."

The half smile on her lips warmed him to the

core as she reached for the tablet. Taking it from him, she swiped her index finger across the screen to review the attachments.

"Anything you think might help the investigation?" she asked. "Or did you happen to solve the entire case and identify the Hunter on your own?"

Declan wiped his overheated palms down his jeans, studied the too-bright screen as she skimmed page after page. "I'm not an investigator, remember? You're asking the wrong guy."

"First impressions. Tell me what you thought when you looked at the crime scene photos." Green eyes sparkled in the glow from the tablet's light as she hiked one shoulder in a shrug. Kate reached to the end table beside the chair he'd taken up and switched on a small lamp. What was this? Some kind of test?

Okay. "The victims might've been hidden enough to keep them from being found too easily, but they were staged."

Something familiar took root from inside him, the need to solve the puzzle as if his life—or someone else's—depended on it. His heart pumped hard behind his rib cage, adrenaline consuming him from head to toe. Declan stood and stepped close to her, his arm brushing against her uninjured side as they reviewed the evidence together. Her touch, like an anchor, kept him in the moment as possibilities of the way the killer hunted his victims played out in his head. He'd lure them in, maybe seduce them, then set them free in the wilderness. Had he given them a head start before he'd started the hunt?

Declan swiped his index finger across the screen and landed on a single photo of one of the crime scenes. Focusing on the surrounding damp ground and not the body where most investigators started, he pointed to a small patch of bare dirt. "See here? There are no footprints in the dirt, nothing to suggest the grass has been disturbed around her. Like she fell from the sky. The killer brought them to those locations and left them to be discovered."

"They were killed elsewhere." Kate nodded as she scrolled to the next attachment. "Makes sense. The lack of blood at the scenes backs up your theory. The victims had to have been placed after they were already dead a few hours, which means these killings were thought out. Meticulously planned ahead of time. The killer knew exactly where their bodies would end up, maybe even when they'd be discovered, because he picked the locations personally."

She was placating him. The excitement drained from his muscles, and he backed off a step. A small burst of laughter escaped as he ran a hand through his hair. The sting of his stitches pulled at him. "None of this is new information, is it?"

"No. But it can't hurt to have a second pair of eyes. There might be something in these files I'm missing that could help me build the profile on the guy." She handed him the tablet, then headed toward the kitchen and flipped on the coffee maker.

Pulling two mugs from one of the cabinets, she set them out as the sound of bubbling water reached his ears. Within a few minutes, she'd poured them two hot cups of coffee.

Green eyes landed on him as she offered the second cup. "I will mention, however, that it took the investigating unit two hours to come up with the same theory that it took you two minutes to put together."

Surprise washed through him. Two hours? Seemed kind of obvious to him. He just had to look at the right evidence. Or had it been his past life as a serial crimes investigator coming into play?

Liquid heat bled through the mug and into his hand. "Dominic barely just sent you the email. How do you know how long it took them?"

"I'm in a group message with the BAU assigned to the case." A smile thinned her lips as she leaned forward, one leg tucked under the other. Her robe shifted, revealing pale, smooth skin above her collar. Under her thin shirt, the scars interrupted that perfection, but they only made her more beautiful in his opinion. Stronger.

She brought the mug to her lips, eyes on him over the rim. "You're good at this, Declan. You always have been. Investigating is in your bones. There's something still there and you know it."

There'd always been something, ever since he'd woken up in that hospital bed, that urged him to take a closer look, to solve the puzzles around him. Seemed the only puzzle he hadn't been able to solve had been his past, but now he was starting to get answers. Because he'd found her. If he could get even an ounce of the life he'd had back, maybe the cold, gnawing hole of emptiness inside would heal. Maybe he could start over.

He focused on the screen in his lap. "Tell me about the Hunter."

"My profile is far from solid. I only have bits and pieces right now." She set her mug on the end table to her left and stood. "Besides, Michaels is still out there. We should be focusing on finding him. His sister took custody of him after his release, and there's only one address on file for her. We should head out at first light. It's about a two-hour drive."

"First impressions." He echoed her own words back to her, drawing out a languid smile as he handed her the tablet.

"All right." Kate stared down at the screen but didn't seem to see the words in front of her. Her bottom lip parted from the top, and everything inside of him heated in an instant. "I think he's punishing her."

"Who?" he asked.

"The woman who broke his heart." She turned the tablet to face him, but he couldn't stand to take another look at the collage of all three victims. It was all too easy to imagine Kate—blond hair, green eyes—staring up at the sky, perfect sensual lips blue, unmoving.

They'd just met. Sure, they'd been married, but as she'd pointed out, he wasn't her husband anymore. He didn't know her, had no attachment to her other than the flashes of memories in his head. But the image of finding her as those women had been found initiated a violent chain reaction inside, starting with his head and working down to his toes.

"He chooses his victims based on *her* appearance," she said. "From the care he's put into placing them, stands to reason he's been intimate with them, maybe even dated them. He seduces his victims, then kills them, gently covering them in grass and foliage to protect their bodies until they're discovered. He can't bear to hurt the one person he wants to, so he replaces her with his victims. He takes his anger with her out on them, but the hurt never stops. No matter how many times he kills, her face is the one he can't forget."

"Then if the FBI can find her, they'll find their serial killer," Declan said. "In a city of three hundred thousand people, should be no problem at all." The excitement was back, stirring something deep within him.

First thing first. They had a shooter to find. Declan clapped his hands then rubbed them together. "Where's that address for Brian Michaels?"

Chapter Six

She couldn't change the past.

Hoping Declan's memories returned—that her husband was still in there, waiting to reemerge—was more dangerous than being in Michaels's sights again. She could heal physically. She'd done it before. But mentally? Kate adjusted her grip on the steering wheel. No. She'd lost him once. If she gave in to the hope buried deep down, she wasn't sure she'd survive the second time.

"You're dead on your feet." Declan's familiar voice charged through her system inside the too-small cabin of the SUV. They'd been driving for two hours, yet every time he spoke was a new lesson in awareness. "Did you actually get any sleep?"

"When you're the possible target of a shooter, sleeping isn't exactly a priority," she said.

Dried foliage and dead twigs crunched beneath the vehicle's tires. Reds, yellows, oranges and browns announced fall had arrived in Alaska as they inched along the dirt road heading away from

Potter Creek Ravine Park, but the dropping temperatures said it wouldn't last long. Snow would cover these parts in the next couple of weeks, if not sooner, which would only make it harder for law enforcement to recover any more of the Hunter's victims and catalog the evidence.

"I've got more important things to worry about," she said.

"Exhaustion is not a badge of honor, Kate, and it sure as hell won't get us to Michaels any faster." Declan shifted his weight in his seat, one hand clamped onto the bullet wound in his side. "Speaking of which, where the hell are we going, and do you have to hit every bump along the way?"

Had that been concern in his voice? A smile spread her lips at the idea, but she forced herself to pay attention to the road and not the way the veins in his arms rippled beneath his skin. She'd been on her own for so long, getting used to someone else's concern would take a while to sink in. Sure, the team had her back. She trusted that any one of them would stand up for her, fight for her, show up if she needed them. But would they have taken a bullet for her as Declan had less than twenty-four hours ago?

"Michaels's sister has a residence about a mile north of here. She's the only living relative he has left, and court documents recorded he was released into her custody." A hard knot of hesitation twisted in her gut. She couldn't ignore the fact Michaels's sister lived only a half mile from one of the crime scenes she'd studied for the Hunter case, but it had to be a coincidence. Nothing more. "If he's hiding out, that's where he'll be."

"You didn't answer my question about the bumps, which makes me think you're hitting them on purpose." Declan stared out the passenger side window, toward the hint of light coming over the Chugach mountain range.

The sun wouldn't rise for another hour, but her brain filled in what she couldn't see of his expression. The laugh line on the left side of his mouth, deeper than the one on the right. The damage he'd done chewing off the skin of his bottom lip. The small dark spot of brown in his right eye. Brains were funny like that. Always trying to fill in the blanks.

"Consider it payback. Before you..." Kate stopped herself from saying the words out loud again. How much more pain could she possibly expect her heart to take?

"We used to prank each other," she said instead. "Small things at first, but over the years, we got a bit more dramatic and tried to top one another. I have to admit, there might've been some pain involved." She couldn't fight the small lift of one corner of her mouth. "The last prank I played, I applied wax to your leg while you were sleeping, then ripped off over half of your leg hair on your thigh. You retaliated by setting my alarm clock to go off every hour for the next two nights."

"Well, that answers the question I had about my uneven leg hair." His deep laugh vibrated through her as he pressed his back into the seat, and every nerve ending she owned heightened in awareness. How long had it been since she'd heard that laugh? But all too soon, it bled into the background of the engine's growl.

"Hard to believe I had a whole life before this," he said. "I can't remember any of it, but you do, and you've had to face it alone. I can't imagine how much strength that took to keep going."

A sharp intake of breath burned her throat, and she sobered instantly. Not strength. Repression. Day in, day out, she committed to becoming a fraction more numb than she'd been the day before. She'd thrown herself into other people's heads, learning their habits, their secrets, *their* pain to keep the grief from carving a bigger hole in her soul. But since he'd walked back into her life, there'd been a spark, a small flame he'd ignited with that kiss, with the way he studied her, cared for her.

"Have you seen a neurologist?" she asked.

"Kind of hard to get an appointment when you don't know your real name, have insurance or employment history," he said. "Or any way to pay for it."

Right.

"I have a friend who works at the Alaska Neurology Center," she said. "She owes me a favor for having the team help her with a case last year. I'm sure she wouldn't mind running some tests. There might be something you could be doing—mental exercises—to speed up the process." Kate didn't think that kind of science existed, but it was worth a shot, wasn't it? "Your memory loss might not be as permanent as you think."

Especially when it came to investigative work.

"Thank you." The weight of his attention pinned her to her seat. "Really. You don't have to be doing any of this."

"Well, I am the reason you got shot in the first place, right?" Hollowness set up residence in the pit of her stomach. Her mouth dried. "I should at least try to make it up to you."

"I told you. Michaels is responsible for his actions," he said. "Not you."

"Doesn't matter what you believe. It's the truth. Maybe if I'd been more focused on Michaels during our sessions, none of this would've happened."

The road wound deeper into the woods, pulling them into darkness. Kate guided the SUV to a stop outside of a short brown wooden fence surrounding the property. "This is it. We're here."

Tufts of green grass sprouted across the half acre of dirt. Dried leaves from the surrounding trees covered the landscape, bare branches hanging dangerously low over the cabin's roof. The weathered planks along the sides of the structure hadn't been repaired, left exposed to the elements for what looked like years. Broken windows reflected the rising sunlight sneaking over the mountain peaks, and from what she could see from here, the front door had been left partially open.

"Are we about to be murdered?" Declan shouldered his way out of the vehicle, leaving the passenger-side door wide-open. "I'm getting the sense your patient isn't here."

"Former patient." Hitting the button to shut off the engine, she rolled her fingers into a fist to control the tremors. She hadn't seen Michaels since his last session, since before… She tucked her bottom lip between her teeth and bit down to keep herself in the moment. One. Two. She could do this. She had to do this.

Kate got out of the SUV, leaves crunching beneath her boots. The small sign nailed to the fence said this was the address on Michaels's release paperwork. Her fingers tingled for her weapon. "This is the address his sister gave the judge."

"I think the judge got played." Declan stepped toward the thigh-high wooden gate protesting at the slightest push of the breeze. "There's nobody here. Are you sure it was his sister who showed up to claim him?"

No. She wasn't. In fact, Michaels had never mentioned a sister in the few sessions she'd had with him. He'd refused to talk about his family, despite her attempt to help him through a sudden emergence of a dissociative disorder.

Before emergency medics had brought him into the ER after he'd attempted suicide, he'd lost his job, his wife had filed for divorce and taken custody of his kids. Statistically, the disorder was brought on by trauma—abuse, combat—but his medical records hadn't shown anything out of the norm and there was no record of him serving in the military. So who would have taken custody of him if they weren't a relative and why?

Her instincts screamed to get out of there as she pushed open the gate, but this was the only lead they had to finding the person who took those shots at them last night. Reaching for her ankle, Kate unholstered the small, loaded revolver she kept as backup. "Here. You might need this."

She wasn't taking the chance of him getting shot again, unholstering her Glock from her shoulder holster.

Declan took the weapon and checked the rounds.

They moved as one toward the cabin. No lights. No fresh tire tracks. No movement. Nothing to suggest the place had been recently occupied, but the weight of being watched aggravated her instincts. If Michaels was the shooter from last night, it stood to reason he wouldn't stop until he was caught or killed. Putting this address on his release papers could've just been a way to draw her into the trap. Bringing the prey to the hunter.

Warmth penetrated through her cargo jacket and settled deep into her bones as she brushed against Declan. She'd trained for situations exactly like this, but having him here, at her side, calmed the raging storm of uncertainty inside. Her mouth tingled with the memory of his bruising kiss, and she took a deep breath to keep herself from analyzing every moment of it.

Despite their personal situation, the plan hadn't changed. She'd find Michaels, help Declan get his life back and move on. End of story.

He positioned himself ahead of her, taking point as though he intended to protect her from any danger that lay ahead. His mountainous shoulders blocked her view into the cabin. "This doesn't feel right."

"I think we've seen enough," she said. Lowering her weapon, she swiped a bead of sweat from her temple with the back of her hand. The temperatures had dropped below freezing out here. How could she possibly be sweating?

Kate surveyed the property a second time. She still couldn't shake the feeling they were being watched, but there was nothing here. And they were out of leads. She took a step back, retreating toward the SUV. "Michaels isn't—"

There was movement to her left, the outline of a man in the trees, but in an instant, he was gone. Kate blinked to clear her vision. Sunlight had barely started lighting the west end of the property. Had it been a trick of the shadows? She searched the tree line. Nothing. She wasn't crazy. He'd been right there.

Shifting off the safety tab on her weapon, she checked back over her shoulder to gauge Declan's reaction. "Did you see that?"

"Sure as hell did." He moved beside her, the

revolver gripped in his hand. Staring toward the spot the shadow had disappeared, he raised the gun. "We're not alone out here after all."

THE SHADOW IN the tree line hadn't been any ghost. With uneven terrain and minimal sunlight coming over those mountains, they were at a disadvantage here. For all Declan knew, the guy in the trees knew every inch of this property and beyond. They needed to call in Kate's team. "Let's get your team on the line—"

"I'm going after him." She moved fast, sprinting across the property, gun in hand.

"Kate!" Damn it. He couldn't let her go after the suspect alone. The fake address, the cabin—it could have been a setup from the beginning.

Declan pumped his legs hard, but all too soon, the stitches in his side ripped. The pain pushed the air from his lungs, but he wouldn't slow down. Not with the chance the bastard was waiting for her to come into range. Someone had already taken a shot at her in the past twenty-four hours. He wouldn't let it happen again.

Broken branches and tall grass threatened to trip him up as she disappeared into the tree line. Panic exploded through his system. Damn. He'd lost sight of her.

Freezing temperatures and the pain in his side battled for his attention, but he only cared about her. Declan pushed himself harder, into the darkness, past the first line of trees. Sunlight lightened the sky enough for him to navigate around a fallen tree ahead of him, but there was no sign of her.

He slowed long enough to take in his surroundings. No beam of flashlight. No sounds of gunshots. Kate had been trained to protect herself, but he'd be damned if he didn't get her out of this mess. He couldn't lose her. Not again. "Kate!"

Rustling reached his ears from the left, and he bolted that direction, his hand slick against the steel of the revolver. A shadow crossed his path ahead, moving fast, with another on its trail. Had to be her.

Gripping his side, Declan launched himself over a small stream cutting through the wilderness. A growl worked up his throat as another stitch tore beneath the gauze, but he swallowed it down as he landed boots first. She wasn't going to get away from him that easily and neither was the bastard she was chasing. Hauling himself upright, he forced himself to keep going. Branches drew blood at his face and arms. "You better be alive when I find you, angel."

He wouldn't lose her again.

The trees shifted to his right, pulling his gaze from the path a split second before a wall of muscle slammed into him. He twisted and fell, rolling into the stream. What the ever loving hell?

Cold water heightened his senses as he planted his hands into the ground and locked on the outline of a man less than ten feet away.

The shadowy bastard had doubled back and lost Kate in the process.

Or there were two of them.

Declan straightened. His attacker blocked Declan's path to Kate, planted himself directly in the center of the trail. It'd been a trap.

Swiping his thumb across the bottom of his nose, he dislodged the water dripping down his face. "All right. Let's get this over with."

The masked assailant charged.

Shifting his weight onto his back foot, Declan caught the bastard just as the shadow's shoulder slammed into his rib cage. Mud and foliage gave way beneath his boots, but he kept himself upright. Declan slammed an elbow into his attacker's spine. Faster than he thought possible, the man wrapped his hands around Declan's thighs and hiked him off his feet. The wall of trees blurred in his vision as he hit the ground, his attacker's weight pinning him to the ground.

Sunlight streaked across the wilderness floor, enough for Declan to realize the shadow above him had pulled back his elbow to strike. He dodged the first punch, but the second landed directly into the mess of blood from the stitches in his side.

As though the son of a bitch had known exactly where to strike.

"You should've stayed dead, Monroe."

The voice was distorted, unrecognizable.

Agony washed over Declan's side, and he couldn't hold back the scream clawing up his throat. He rammed his knee into his attacker's side, dislodging him long enough to gain the upper hand.

Adrenaline burned through him, pushed the pain to the back of his mind and cut the last remains of his control. Blood slipped into the waistband of his jeans as he rocketed his fist into the masked bastard's face. Twice more.

But Declan wasn't through yet. Grabbing his attacker's collar in one hand, he positioned his arm for another hit. The shadow wobbled on his knees, barely upright. The suspect Kate had gone chasing after must've been a decoy. "Give it up, Michaels. You're finished, and you will never get your hands on her."

A low, uneven laugh bled through the pounding heartbeat in his ears. Clamping one gloved hand over Declan's, the masked assailant pried the grip from his collar and rose. Toe-to-toe, his attacker reached well over Declan's six-foot-two.

"Even with a second chance at a new life, you couldn't leave well enough alone, could you? You always had to be the hero."

What? Narrowing his eyes, Declan fought against the strength twisting his wrist, but the mask didn't reveal any identifying characteristics. Hell, even if it did, he wasn't sure he'd have anything to compare them to. The amnesia had stymied any chance of that. But the suspect in front of him didn't come across as a former patient diagnosed with dissociative disorder. No. This man had training, military or law enforcement if Declan had to guess. He was in control. A predator. A killer. "You're not Michaels. Who the hell are you?"

"Doesn't matter who I am." A fast strike to the solar plexus shot the nerves there into overdrive, pressurized his lungs, and Declan fell to one knee. The pain in his arm intensified as the shadow above held on to his hand. Any wrong move and the bones would shatter. The suspect had him in the perfect position to take him out of the fight altogether, and he knew it. "But you. You're just in my way."

Kate.

Every cell in his body heated. Declan craned back his head, attention focused on the bastard's dark gaze burning down on him. He ignored the pain in his side and his wrist. He'd been through worse, recovered from worse. And there was no way in hell the son of a bitch would touch Kate. "As long as I'm alive, you'll never get to her."

"I can fix that." His attacker increased the pressure.

Declan came up swinging. He landed a solid hit with his nondominant hand, hauling the SOB to the left and exposing his assailant's back. With a hard kick to the attacker's knee, Declan followed through with his elbow to the base of the neck, but the guy didn't stay down for long.

The bastard struck fast.

Declan wrapped his hand around the attacker's wrist, raised his arm over his head and targeted the man's rib cage. Once. Twice.

The woods blended into a stream of lifeless color as Declan was shoved forward into the bark of a wide pine. Agonizing pain ripped through him from his gunshot wound, and Declan dropped to his knees. Clinging to the tree in front of him, he fought to stay upright as darkness closed in around the edges of his vision.

His attacker moved into his peripheral vision, a black shadow in a forest of brightening light. Fisting his hand in Declan's hair, he wrenched his head back as a hint of sunlight gleamed off metal. A knife. "To think, all this time, I thought you'd be hard to kill."

Blood dripped onto the dried leaves beneath him, a soft pattering in his ears. Declan clutched his side to slow the blood flow, but his heart was pumping too hard, too fast. Depending on the damage, he'd bleed out in a matter of minutes if he didn't get medical help. But not before he got to Kate. "Go to hell."

"See you there." The knife came at him fast, but Declan rolled at the last second.

His assailant's scream penetrated through the thick haze clouding Declan's head as the blade slashed across his upper thigh. Declan pushed to his feet, facing off with the masked thug and the large serrated hunting knife. Stinging pain spread through his skull, but a few hairs in the name of survival weren't anything to miss.

His strength drained with every drop of blood hitting the ground, but the moment Declan backed down, his attacker would go after Kate. Not happening. She'd already been through hell. He wasn't going to give this bastard the power to break her again. The past, his memories. None of it mattered right now. She mattered.

He struggled to stay balanced, blinked to clear the sweat from his eyes and raised his fists. The pristine edge of the blade had been tainted with the attacker's own blood. "Want to take bets on which one of us bleeds out faster?"

"I've already won." The man lunged, a grunt filling the silence of the woods around them.

The knife made contact with Declan's arm and tore through his T-shirt into skin. He blocked the second strike, dodged the third. Throwing his weight into his arm, Declan pushed off the tree behind him and swung as hard as he could. Bone met bone, a satisfying crack. He followed the blade's path into the group of dying brush, wrapped his fingers around the handle and turned back to finish the fight.

He wasn't fast enough.

Clamping his hands on either side of Declan's head, his assailant pulled Declan's face directly into his knee.

Lightning flashed across the backs of his eyes as the world tilted on its axis. The blade fell from his hand as his legs dropped out from under him. He collapsed to his side, watching as his attacker collected the knife. His limbs refused to obey his brain's commands as the son of a bitch centered himself in Declan's darkening vision.

"I'm going to find her, Monroe. I'm going to

make her pay for what she's done." The mask stretched thin across the lower half of the attacker's face, as though he were smiling beneath it. "And there's nothing you can do to stop me."

"No." Declan clawed at the dirt and leaves as the man walked away. He had to get up. He had to fight. But the darkness sucked him down.

Chapter Seven

Kate had closed in right on the shadow's tail, gun in hand.

Only now she recognized the build, the grayish-blond hair, the terrified features as he chanced a glance back at her. Brian Michaels. Branches and needles whipped at her face, but with the rising sun, there was little chance of losing him, even in the dense trees. How far were they from the cabin now? Half a mile? More? Her muscles burned with exhaustion, her lungs on fire from the frozen temperatures. "Brian, stop!"

Ten feet. She pumped her legs as fast as she could. Five feet. She could almost reach out and touch him. Kate stretched her hand forward, fingers brushing the soft fabric of his sweatshirt hood—

Her foot tangled in the bushes, and she hit the ground hard. A combination of pain and relief coursed through her muscles as she forced herself to look up. Michaels raced away from her, his footsteps fading within a few seconds. Tightening her hold on the gun, she pulled at her boot to get free of whatever'd she gotten caught it in. "Damn it."

Moisture soaked through her jeans and T-shirt as she sat up. If she hurried, she could still catch up with Michaels, but her foot wouldn't come loose. A flash of yellow revealed why.

Kate reholstered her weapon beneath her jacket. The crime scene tape woven throughout the dried weeds had caught in the metal brackets of her boots. She picked at it until she slid her foot out but didn't drop the thin plastic as she straightened. "What would crime scene tape be doing all the way out here?"

Surveying the trees, the surrounding grass, she froze. She knew this area, had seen dozens of photos of it, had memorized it to ensure she hadn't missed a single element of evidence when she'd started profiling the Hunter. Blood drained from her face, and cold worked through her "This is where they found her."

The first victim.

Had to be a coincidence. Kate released the tape, letting it settle back into the bushes and took a single step forward. Unless...

She spun, searching the surrounding trees for signs of movement. No. Michaels didn't fit the profile. The evidence at all three scenes spoke of undeniable, unfulfilled rage that only grew with every kill, but the murders had been planned down to the very last detail. The FBI's suspect was a psychopath. Not a sociopath. He could control his emotions, hold on to them until the job was done.

Michaels couldn't string two sentences together before his disorder got the better of him. The Hunter stalked his victims, seduced them, then brought them out to the woods and hunted them for sport. Each kill had been too organized. Too detailed. Nothing like her former patient.

Then again, her entire job was to deal in opinions. One wrong assumption and an entire case could unravel.

Kate trudged through the knee-high grass, leaving the scene behind. Everything had been processed by the FBI. There was nothing left for her to analyze. Now she just had to figure out a way out of here and relocate Michaels. "Declan!"

She could've sworn he'd been right behind her. He could be anywhere now. Spinning in a complete circle, she headed west across the small open field she hadn't realized she'd run through during her pursuit of Michaels.

She'd find Michaels again. There were only so many places a man like that could go, and one day he'd make a mistake. She'd be there when he did. The bullet graze across her arm itched. She was tired of getting shot at. "Decl—"

Another flash of color caught her eye. Red this time. Kate slowed, her fingers tingling for her weapon as she proceeded through the grass. Pine cones beneath her boots broke the uneasy silence around her as she unholstered her weapon again. What were the chances…

No. Couldn't be.

The wind picked up, the undeniable scent of perfume on the air, and her stomach revolted. Pale skin and blond hair stood stark against the browns, reds and greens of the surrounding foliage as she came around a thicket of grass. The sun was high enough now to highlight the soft gleam of the red silk dress draped across the woman. The woman with an arrow in her chest.

Kate wrenched herself away from the scene as fast as she could to avoid contaminating the evidence. The shrimp linguine Declan had taken such care to make rushed up her throat, emptying her stomach in a matter of seconds.

Her heart pounded too loud behind her ears. A light breeze wove through the trees. One breath. Two. Didn't help. She could still smell the woman's perfume, still see those green eyes staring up at her. She had to call Special Agent Dominic.

The Hunter had struck again.

Shoving her hand in her jacket pocket, she gripped the phone and tapped the screen. No service. She wiped her mouth with the back of her hand. Every minute the scene waited to be discovered, evidence disappeared. Storms, wildlife. She couldn't leave the poor girl out here alone, but unless Declan found her on his own, Kate would have to trek east back through the woods to the SUV. She forced one foot in front of the other toward the woman in the red dress, covering her mouth with her hand.

The woman fit the appearance of the Hunter's three other victims. Around thirty years old, blond hair, green eyes, athletic from the look of her frame and bare shoulders. She hadn't been out here long. Maybe a couple hours judging by the presence of color beneath the skin. A fresh kill.

Kate had joined Blackhawk Security and consulted with the FBI to prevent things like this from happening. Maybe if she'd started the profile sooner...

She closed her eyes. No. Evidence suggested the Hunter seduced his victims days in advance. This one had been chosen long before the FBI and Dominic's team had sent her the files. Kate stared at the woman's hands, pale against the backdrop of her dress, then focused on the victim's face. Memorized it. "I'm going to find him. I promise. Whoever did this to you is going to—"

Green eyes blinked back at her.

A scream escaped her control. Kate pushed away, the heel of her boot catching on a rock, and she landed hard on her back. Her breath came in small gasps as the last of her adrenaline coursed through her. Running her hand through her hair, she fumbled for her phone again—still no service—and crouched beside the woman.

The victim wasn't dead. The arrow must've missed her heart. "Hang on," Kate said. "I'm going to get you help. Can you tell me your name?"

The breath wheezed from between the woman's chapped lips. "M…ary."

"Mary." No time for more questions. Kate had to get help. Placing one hand just below where the arrow entered Mary's chest, she hit the power button on her phone five times and swiped her thumb across the screen to report her location to law enforcement. She retrieved the Blackhawk Security earpiece all operatives were required to carry from the bottom of her jacket pocket and secured it in her ear.

"I won't leave you, okay? Hang on, Mary. Help is on the way," Kate said. "Sullivan—anybody—do you hear me? I need an ambulance sent to my location."

Static reached through the earbud. Out of range. Kate wrapped her hand around Mary's and gave a soft squeeze. The fear in the victim's eyes speared straight through her. "I'm not going anywhere, but I don't have service in this spot. I need to walk around for a minute. I promise I'll be right back. I won't leave you."

Standing, she raised her phone above her head, hoping to catch a stray signal as she walked away a few steps. Where the hell was Declan? She slowed, cocking her head back over her shoulder toward Mary. If the Hunter had just deposited his latest kill—who wasn't dead yet—there was a chance…

The control she'd fought so hard to put back in place after Declan had stripped her bare cracked.

"Where are you?" she asked.

Something was wrong. Declan had been almost right behind her as she pursued Michaels through the woods.

A soft whistling broke through the silence. She searched the tree line, took a single step forward as every cell in her body tensed to that sound.

Pain erupted through her shoulder.

The momentum of the arrow wrenched her sideways, and she hit the ground. Her phone disappeared into the grass, shock overriding her normally quick reaction time.

She tried to sit up as blood trickled across her collarbone and over her neck. Biting back the scream building in her throat, she used her uninjured arm to flip onto her stomach and army crawl back toward Mary. The arrow's fletching scraped against the dirt, caught on weeds, and only intensified the agony ripping through her, but she'd keep her promise. She wasn't going to leave Mary out here alone. "Mary, we have to move."

They had to get out of here.

No answer.

The taste of copper and salt strengthened as she neared the Hunter's latest victim. Blood. The nausea churning in her gut drowned the pain for just a moment.

Mary stared straight up at the sky. No movement. No chest sounds. Nothing.

Kate's eyes burned as she wrapped her hand in the woman's once again, almost shaking her. No. No, no, no, no. She blinked against the rush of dizziness threatening to pull her under, her body growing heavier by the minute. "Mary."

Footsteps thundered through grass and dirt, loud above the frantic beat of her heart. The Hunter closing in on his prey.

She shuddered as she unholstered the gun from under her jacket. Kate ensured she'd already loaded a round. Forget the shooting. Forget the mind-screwing situation with Declan. Forget the profile. The only thing that mattered now was survival.

Because she sure as hell wasn't about to be the Hunter's next victim.

DECLAN WOULD FIND HER, or he'd die trying.

Mud gave way beneath his boots as he stumbled forward, one hand clutching his side. His shoulder rammed into a tree beside him, and he struggled to catch his breath. He didn't know how long he'd been unconscious, how much blood he'd lost. Didn't matter. He promised Kate he'd protect her, and that was exactly what he was going to do.

He strengthened his grip around the large hunting knife he'd recovered from the bushes. The bastard wouldn't lay a finger on her.

Pulling his hand back away from the wound, he stared at the bright red across his fingers, then wiped it down his jeans. He pushed himself forward, muscles begging for relief as he followed the footprints along the thin trail. The sun had risen fully, almost a bright tunnel of light straight ahead as though he were being led through the trees. A ring of black closed in around his vision, and he slowed to use a tree for support. Damn it. He'd lost too much blood. Soon, his organs would start shutting down one by one.

He had to find her before that.

"I'm coming for you, angel. Hang on, baby." Air wheezed up his throat as he soldiered forward. He'd been through—survived—worse. A single gunshot wound was nothing compared to the four he'd taken a year ago. Then again, he'd been treated by an entire team of medical professionals, he'd been declared dead by the end of surgery and he hadn't been chasing a psychopath through the woods where all kinds of infections lay in wait. "I'm coming."

If the psycho hurt her…

Rage—explosive and hot—burned through him. His assailant thought he knew him? Whoever'd attacked him had no idea what kind of monster he'd kept caged all this time. How much anger, hatred and bitterness he carried from having everything ripped away. But Declan was more than happy to show him.

A twig snapped nearby, and Declan slowed. The hairs on the back of his neck stood on end, and he turned from the edge of the meadow. No movement, but the feeling he was being watched only intensified. Strangled breathing reached his ears, pulling him to the right. The blade grew heavy in his hand as exhaustion sucked the life from his body, but he'd still do the job.

"I know you're there," he rasped. "Come out so we can finish this."

No answer.

"Kate?" His defenses dropped as panic consumed him. Had the bastard already gotten to her? The breathing grew stronger as Declan rushed around to the other side of a massive tree. His heart beat hard behind his rib cage as a pair of boots came into sight. He slowed. A pair of men's boots.

Brian Michaels. Blood from a wound in his neck stained the collar of a bright white shirt beneath his dark sweatshirt. Blue eyes called out for help. Kate's former patient had already lost too much.

Declan took a single step forward, biting down against the rush of pain in his side, and stabbed the knife straight down into the dirt. The muscles ticked in his jaw as he crouched in front of Michaels and ripped off his own shirt. He tried plugging the flow of blood with the fabric, but it was too late. Michaels had been sentenced to death the second his throat had been cut. Blood slipped from Michaels's fingers as he reached out to Declan.

"I should kill you right now." Declan could put him out of his misery. Walk away and let whatever higher power out there decide what to do with the man. Michaels was the one who took those shots a year ago. He'd done this to Declan's memory. Taken Kate's husband from her, taken their baby and ruined their lives.

But the thought of finishing the job only hollowed Declan's gut more. He curled his fingers around the blade, drawing Michaels's gaze. "You took everything from her."

Michaels's jaw worked overtime as he set his head back against the tree bark. The shooter's graying hair and beard added to the lack of color overtaking his features. This wasn't the man who'd attacked him back in the woods. "Hired…me."

Cold worked through Declan. "Who?"

Michaels's shoulders pulsed with shallow breaths. "He'll…kill—"

"You're saying someone hired you to shoot Kate?" Hell. Declan increased the pressure on the bastard's wound. No. Michaels wasn't going to die out here. Not when they were so close to uncovering the truth. That was too easy. He deserved a life of guilt knowing how many lives he'd destroyed.

"Tell me who sent you after Kate Monroe, and I'll make sure you're put in the FBI's protective witness program." All Declan needed was a name—anything he could go off of—to end this nightmare. "He'll never get to you, Brian. I give you my word. Now tell me—"

"Already found…her." Air escaped past Michaels's lips, brown eyes staring into the trees ahead as his chest deflated.

"Michaels, stay with me. Where is she? Where is Kate?" Declan shook the body.

His head pounded as he slid back onto his heels. He threw his blood-soaked shirt to the ground. Damn it. Studying the wound on the shooter's neck, he shut down a shiver working up his spine with a rush of breeze taking his body heat.

Michaels had been the only lead they'd had. There was no doubt in Declan's mind that Kate's former patient had fired those shots last night—just as he had a year ago—but if Declan were to believe a dead man's dying words, a variable had been added. Michaels had been paid to pull the trigger both times. A contract hit.

What were the chances the shooter had died within minutes of Kate and Declan discovering his location?

Two gunshots exploded from nearby.

"Kate." Declan shoved to his feet, knife in hand. Desperation clawed through him as he burst from the tree line and into a wide space of tall grass. The sudden strike of sunlight blinded him, but he pushed himself harder. He wasn't going to lose her. Not again. Because no matter how many times he'd tried to convince himself he'd only stuck around to remember the past, he knew the truth. He didn't give a damn about his memories right now. She was all that mattered. He wasn't going to stop fighting for her.

A scream rang out off to his left, freezing him from the inside. Declan pumped his arms hard. "Kate!"

The masked man who'd attacked him spun around, pulling Kate with him. He was heading toward the trees. Kate struggled in his hold as Declan closed in, her scream still fresh in his mind.

His chest burned with exhaustion. Fifty feet. Forty. The minute the attacker disappeared into the trees, there was a chance Declan would never see her again, a chance she'd become a victim.

Not happening. Adrenaline coursed through him as a hint of her blond hair swung into view. No. He'd been given a gift when she walked back into his life, a second chance. Nobody would take her away from him.

"Come any closer and I will end her right in front of you." The man wrenched Kate close to his body, using her as a shield, his hand gripped around an arrow close to her heart. "Stay where you are, Monroe."

"Tell me you're the one who shot her with an arrow, so I can rip you apart with my bare hands," Declan said, his lungs burning.

Hundreds of crime scene photos pushed to the front of his mind. The victims who looked like Kate with their blond hair and green eyes, the arrows shot through the heart and the bodies left in the woods to be discovered later. As though their killer was punishing the one woman he couldn't make himself hurt, the woman who'd broken his heart. Clearly the killer was highly intelligent, extremely organized and meticulous, knowledgeable of crime scene analysis and police investigations to succeed at staying anonymous this long.

Declan locked his eyes on Kate's, noted the undeniable pain in her expression, then focused on the suspect. "You're the Hunter."

"Declan, get out of here—" Another scream ripped up her throat as her captor twisted the arrow deeper into her shoulder.

Her agony seared into Declan's brain. He'd never forget that sound. Fire burned through his veins, and he took another step forward, fists clenched. He forced his jaw to release. "You're going to want to start running."

"One more step and she dies, remember?" The Hunter reached into his cargo pants pocket and extracted what looked like a car remote. "Besides, I think you'll be too busy trying to save yourself."

He hit the button.

A metal length of barbed wire tightened around both of Declan's feet, tearing through his jeans and deep into muscle. Pain exploded from his ankles as a mechanical hiss pulled Declan's gaze to the left. A groan worked up his throat. He reached down to relieve the pressure, but the world tilted on its axis as the trap pulled tight and hefted him higher.

"No!" Kate lunged for the trap's trigger, only to be ripped back into the Hunter's chest by her hair. "Declan!"

He reached to pry the oversize snare trap from his legs, but gravity and the fact he'd already lost too much blood stripped his strength. Droplets hit the bottom of his chin as he reached again. He couldn't get loose. Not with his body going into shock from blood loss and not without putting Kate at a greater risk of danger.

"Don't worry, Monroe. I have a feeling you won't

be in pain much longer." The Hunter closed in on his newest prey, hand back on that damn arrow in Kate's shoulder.

Sweat pooled at the base of Declan's spine as the bastard stared up at him.

"I'm going…to kill you." Declan blinked to clear his head. To memorize every inch of Kate's face before he blacked out again. As soon as he got out of this trap, he'd start a hunt of his own. Black spiderwebs crossed his vision as Kate slumped in her attacker's arms, unconscious.

"We'll see." The Hunter adjusted quickly, tossing her over his shoulder in a fireman's hold. "After all, you do keep surprising me."

Chapter Eight

No one could hear her screams.

She didn't know how long she'd been down here, unconscious, but her throat hurt from the effort, and the darkness had crept in. Still, no one had come for her. The combination of damp earth and salt dove deep in her lungs. Her fingers were sore—possibly bloodied—from clawing at the dirt walls, but with the arrow in her shoulder, she hadn't been able to climb. With the tarp above, she couldn't see well enough to determine what else could be down here. The man who'd taken her—the Hunter—had tossed her into a pit trap and left her to die.

She screamed again, her throat raw. She closed her eyes against her last memories of Declan. There'd been so much blood. His face had been covered in it. Was he still alive? Had he gotten free? Had he gotten help?

Kate forced herself to breathe evenly, to consider the situation rationally. She wasn't going to run out of air down here, and the tarp overhead would keep most of the elements at bay, but she could starve. She could die of dehydration.

Rubbing at her throat, she sank back on her heels. From what she could tell, the circular pit was about ten feet in diameter and ten feet deep. No branches or roots protruding from the sides to help her climb, but the pain in her shoulder combined with the loss of blood had only let her survey half of the hole so far.

Screaming wouldn't help. She was trapped. Like an animal.

"Think." She had to control the fear skirting up her spine. Deep breath through her nose, exhale through her mouth. The tension burrowing in her neck almost released. Almost.

The Hunter didn't want her dead. At least, not yet. Why else would he have shielded his face and disguised his voice? Which meant he'd been reacting to having her at the scene of his last kill. He hadn't planned for her, but if she didn't get herself out of here, she was going to die. He'd only stashed her here until he could figure out what to do with her or until he could come back. But Kate didn't want to die.

She felt around, her fingers brushing against a large rock that barely fit in the palm of her hand. She couldn't do anything until she dealt with the arrow in her shoulder. Wiping her damp palm on her jeans, she clutched the rock as hard as she could. The arrow hadn't gone all the way through. She couldn't pull it out without tearing through more tendon and muscle and possibly damaging her shoulder permanently.

Tapping her head back against the wall of dirt behind her, she closed her eyes. Declan was out there, alone, bleeding. He needed her to get out of this hole, and no matter how many times she'd tried telling herself differently, she needed him. Needed his concern, his touch. She needed that gut-wrenching smile. The only way she'd get to experience any of those things again was to force the arrow all the way through her shoulder. "You can do this."

Most arrow fletchings were super glued to the end of the shaft. This one was made from feathers. Flexible enough to travel through the hole she was about to tunnel into her shoulder if she needed. Holding the rock straight ahead, she positioned it until one smooth side slid against the end of the shaft. Three. Kate swallowed the sudden dryness in her throat. Two. Deep breath. One. She slammed the rock into the arrow as hard as she could.

A strained scream ripped through her as metal pierced through flesh for the second time in a span of a few hours. She battled to stay conscious as darkness cut across her vision, and she dropped the rock beside her. Her lungs worked overtime to keep up with her racing heartbeat.

The woods went utterly silent above the tarp, then slowly came back to life as she remembered to breathe. Leaning forward, she winced as the arrowhead pulled against smaller roots and dirt at her back. She'd pinned herself to the dirt wall by forcing the head of the arrow through, but now she had to separate the arrow tip from the shaft. Still pinned, she wrenched her shoulder away from the wall. Reaching back, her fingers shook as she slipped the edge of the arrowhead. In a few turns, the blood-coated metal dropped away, and she was able to maneuver the shaft back through the entry wound.

"Stay awake. You've got to stay awake." She discarded the shaft of the arrow. Damp earth gave way beneath her boots as she pushed away from the wall, but she sank immediately back to the ground in the middle of the pit. Tightening her hold in the fine labyrinth of roots in the pit floor, she pressed her forehead to the cool dirt.

No, she had to move to the edges, had to find something sturdy to grab on to to pull herself up. Couldn't think about the physics of holding her own weight with one good arm right now. She had to try.

Muted beams of moonlight penetrated through one edge of the tarp above, but not enough for her to see. How long had she been down here? Six hours? More? Stiffness worked through her fingers as temperatures dropped, but she kept moving, kept searching. There had to be something—anything—she could use to pull herself up. "Come on."

Her boot caught on rogue roots at her feet, and she pitched sideways, landing directly on top of something soft, yet solid. The smell of salt tickled her nose as she struggled to sit up. Salt and... cologne?

Supporting herself with her good arm, she fisted

her hands in what felt like wet T-shirt material. What the hell? The Hunter wouldn't have left supplies. The tarp shifted from above, allowing more light into the pit, and horror flooded her.

Shoving back as fast as she could, Kate didn't stop until her back hit the other side of the hole. Air pressurized in her lungs, but it couldn't distract her from the sight of a dead body.

Another victim of the Hunter?

The wetness on his shirt… Blood. Kate rubbed her palms into the dirt, frantically trying to wipe it away. Rationally, she knew it wouldn't do any good, but rationale had gone out the window the minute she'd been thrown in a pit. She was a prisoner for however long the Hunter wanted to keep her.

Tears burned her cheeks as the soft settling of snowflakes on the tarp filled her ears. Michaels's hideout was located far outside Porter Creek's limits. Nobody was coming to save her. Nobody would hear her screaming. Nobody walked these woods at night. She was on her own.

Too many bodies. The first three, then that poor woman in the field. Mary. And now another body here in the pit with her. Kate had dropped her phone and her gun in the grass when the Hunter had shot her. Had any of her emergency tactics gone through so law enforcement could find the Hunter's latest trophy?

She shook her head, wiped at her face with the back of her hand. Didn't matter right now. It wasn't a coincidence her former patient had been out here the same time the Hunter had made his latest kill. They were connected.

She needed to know how. She would not give up. "Get up, Monroe."

She had to finish searching for something to pull herself out. The body lay straight ahead. As much as the thought sickened her, she could use the victim as a sort of stepping stool to higher ground, a branch or root just out of reach. She followed the curve of the pit trap back around until her boot hit the sickeningly familiar feel of the corpse's bloated middle.

Moonlight shifted around the edges of the tarp, and Kate froze. Recognition flared, and her heart rate quickened. The gash across his neck revealed the cause of death, and those wide brown eyes... She was staring at Brian Michaels. The shooter she'd been desperately trying to locate was right in front of her. Only... "The Hunter found you first."

He'd made sure Michaels would never pull a trigger again.

Was she supposed to feel bad about that? Goose bumps prickled across her skin. She couldn't look away from the body at her feet. Couldn't force herself to feel...anything. Leveling her chin, she reached for the wall of dirt for balance as she stepped onto Michaels's torso. Snowflakes worked through the edges of the flapping tarp from above, catching in her eyelashes as she skimmed her fingers over the wall.

Her palm brushed over a large, protruding root, and she latched on with her uninjured hand as tight as she could. She held back the sob of relief swelling inside. She had to keep it together. At least long enough to get out of this hole, long enough until she found Declan. Then she'd trek back to the SUV, call for backup and lead the search team back for Mary's and Michaels's bodies.

She lifted one boot and slammed it into the wall for leverage. Wrapping the root around her forearm, Kate tested her weight. It held, but the tricky part came next. She bit back the groan clawing up her throat as she raised her injured arm overhead. She gripped the root hard and hauled herself up the wall of dirt, slid her hands higher and did it again. Pain ripped through her shoulder, sweat beaded above her furrowed eyebrows and dripped down her spine, but she only pushed herself harder. She was almost there. A cold breeze grazed across the back of her hands as she reached the top of the root, a sensation she'd never take for granted again.

One more foot until she reached the top of the pit. That was all it would take—

The root broke free from the wall and then she was falling. "No!"

She hit the ground hard, the air knocked from her lungs. Her lungs spasmed until she finally gulped enough oxygen to clear the shock.

The edge of the tarp above fluttered with a gust of wind, then rolled back to expose her and Michaels to the elements. Snow fell in a heavy layer now, homing her attention to the root still clutched in her hand. That was her last chance of getting out.

Flakes melted against her skin as she lay there. She barely had the strength to lift her head, let alone try to climb the wall again, but she wouldn't die down here.

She hadn't survived three bullets wounds, a miscarriage and a year's worth of grief over losing her husband to die in the bottom of a pit. She'd fight. She'd find Declan. She'd get the Hunter's victims the justice they deserved. She didn't know how to give up.

Rolling to her side, Kate shoved to her feet, approached the wall and pulled in a long, slow breath. "Help!"

"CUT HIM DOWN!" an unfamiliar voice shouted. "And find Kate!"

White light brightened the backs of his eyelids, and he forced himself to open his eyes. Hands hanging over his head, he blinked to clear the haze. Five beams of light bounced in front of him. Or was it ten?

"Her phone pinged over by that fallen tree. Vincent, you're with me." Female voice this time. Recognition flared as two flashlight beams swung off to his right. Elizabeth Dawson?

"Declan, you alive?" Sullivan Bishop appeared in front of him, the reflective light from Blackhawk Security founder's flashlight deepening the very serious creases in his forehead.

"As far…as I can tell." The words barely slipped from his frozen lips. The last thing he remembered was trying to reach the knife he'd dropped when the trap had hung him upside down. After that… He couldn't remember. Which wasn't a new feeling. "Where's… Kate?"

"We're looking for her." Sullivan twisted around as another flashlight closed in. This one belonging to Anthony Harris. "Give me your knife. I need you to catch him when I cut the line."

"How did you…know…" Declan's body urged him to close his eyes, but he fought against the drugging effect of the cold. They hadn't found Kate yet. The second her team cut him down, he'd go out and look for her. He wouldn't stop until he found her.

"Kate hit the emergency settings on her phone, which pinged Anchorage PD and us. We came as soon as we got the call. Police are searching the cabin where you and Kate left the SUV. We came straight here." Sullivan disappeared from Declan's peripheral vision. The sound of something scratching against tree bark filled his ears. Sullivan was climbing the tree holding Declan hostage. "What the hell happened to my profiler?"

"He took her." Another storm of rage exploded through Declan, but he couldn't act on it. He couldn't do anything right now, but the bastard would pay for every broken hair on her head. Declan guaranteed it. "He took her. I tried to stop him. I wasn't fast enough."

"We'll find her." Sullivan's voice dipped into

dangerous territory. "Trust me. This is what we do best."

"I'm trying to come up with a reason you're still alive with that much blood on you." Anthony took position directly under Declan's shoulders. "Why is it every time we meet, you're literally dying?"

"You got a better...first impression...in mind?" Every breath was agony. Cold worked through him, and the loss of blood didn't help. The wound in his side had gone numb a while ago. Hell, he didn't know how long he'd been strung up like an animal. How long had Kate been missing? Declan rolled his fingers into fists. To prove he had the strength. "I need to find her."

"You need an ambulance." The branch wrapped with trapping line bounced as Sullivan pushed out farther, knife in hand. The flashlight in his mouth skimmed over Declan's face, and Declan blinked at the sudden brightness. "You can't do anything for Kate if you're dead."

"I'm not leaving her out here alone." No way in hell. He'd made her a promise. He wasn't going anywhere until she was in his arms. Forget an ambulance. Forget the investigation. Forget the past. Declan needed to find her.

"Get ready to grab him, Anthony." The line swayed with Sullivan's efforts to cut through it. What the hell had the Hunter used? Whale line? "He's going to come down hard, and Kate might kill us herself if she finds out we let him die on our watch."

"Please drop me. I'd like…to see that." Declan braced for impact a split second before the line snapped. His shoulder slammed into Anthony's, but the former Ranger flipped him to his feet as though Declan's two hundred pounds—minus at least a liter of blood—meant nothing.

The world swayed, and he stumbled forward but quickly steeled himself. He'd been shot and left upside down for dead, but he wasn't going to give her team any reason to leave him behind during the search. "Thanks."

"Don't mention it." Anthony slipped a pair of brown aviator glasses over his eyes, voice low and even, then unholstered the gun from his shoulder holster. "Ever."

"Here, cover up." Sullivan tossed him a shirt.

"We've got something!" a voice shouted, followed by heavy breathing and footsteps. Elizabeth materialized out of the darkness, but her tone of voice indicated it wasn't because she had good news. "You're going to want to see this, boss."

Sullivan followed without a word, Declan on his trail with Anthony's support. Tall grass and weeds parted as they made their way toward Vincent Kalani's flashlight. Then he noted nothing but red silk.

A body.

"I'd say she died around the same time Kate pinged us with her phone. Six hours, give or take thirty minutes." Vincent moved his flashlight over a woman partially hidden beneath a bed of leaves and pine cones. Tossing something at his boss, the forensics expert crouched beside the victim and pointed west. "I found Kate's phone a few feet away in the grass over there. Must've hit the emergency signal when she found the body."

Sullivan checked the phone. "Then we can't track her with her phone. We'll have to go in blind. Anthony, you're with me." Sullivan tapped his earpiece and searched the tree line where Declan had been hung up to die. "Elliot, quit messing with the damn trap and find something we can track. Vincent, stay with the victim until Anchorage PD or the FBI can take custody. Liz, I want a map of this area on my phone in the next thirty seconds. We're going after Kate."

"I'm…coming, too," Declan said.

Blond hair, green eyes staring straight into the sky, athletic build. Declan's stomach lurched. He didn't give a damn how much blood he'd lost. This victim was one of the Hunter's. Serials usually had a cooling-off period, a time frame while they enjoyed their latest conquest. But not this one. Both this woman and Michaels had died at the Hunter's hand today. Kate wouldn't be next.

Blinking through another round of dizziness, Declan accepted Elizabeth's offered water bottle and downed as much liquid as he could take. "He shot her with an arrow. She's bleeding. You need as many eyes as you can get out there."

"Why do I have the feeling you won't take no for an answer?" Sullivan pegged him with that sea-blue gaze, then extracted a backup weapon, handing it to Declan grip first.

"Let's roll out." Declan checked the weapon, loaded a round into the chamber. One way or another, he was getting Kate back. "She's been gone too long as it is."

The team didn't need any more motivation than that, taking positions. Declan headed for Elliot's flashlight beam at the edge of the woods, checking the time on his wrist. Six hours. That was how long she'd been gone. Anything could've happened in that time, but his gut said she was still alive. She was out there. He ignored the burn of his damaged skin thawing around the wound. Nothing would stop him from finding her.

"Over here! Looks like she put up quite the fight." Elliot swung his flashlight beam straight at them, then back into the heavy shadows as they approached. "Into the woods I go, to lose my mind—"

"—and find my soul," Declan finished.

An apt quote. Because Kate wasn't anything less. She'd been part of him from the beginning, the missing piece. Always would be.

Declan studied the tracks, fresh drag marks leading deeper into the wilderness. He avoided stepping directly on them to preserve the evidence. The minute the news of the Hunter's latest victim hit, the FBI would descend. And he wasn't about to mess up any chance his former employer had of taking this suspect down.

The drag marks disappeared about fifty feet in

from the field, leaving only one set of boot prints. The Hunter had carried her from here, but he had rushed this one. Her abduction hadn't been planned, and he'd made mistakes along the way. He'd left evidence. "This way. Stay sharp. This bastard…is good at what he does."

Declan took point at the head of their pack. Every sound, every movement raised his awareness to another level. This was what the FBI had trained him for, what he'd been good at before the shooting. There were some things he'd never forget. Hunting was one of them.

A few branches off to his right had snapped at the ends, as though someone had broken them on the way through these parts of the woods. He headed that direction.

"You sure you know where you're going?" Sullivan asked.

"Yes." Positive. Kate was counting on him. And there was no way in hell he'd let her down again. Declan slowed as silence descended. What were the chances every animal had vacated the area at the same time? Unless… He pulled up one hand, signaling the team to stop. And listened.

"Help!"

He jerked at that scream, as if he'd been struck by lightning.

"Kate." Declan surged straight ahead, leaving the Blackhawk team behind. Lights swept the area ahead of him and reflected off what looked like a tarp buried with leaves. Fresh snow crunched beneath his boots as he slid to a stop at the edge of a man-made pit in the middle of the woods.

Declan ripped back the tarp, shone his light down into the hole. And there, at the edge, Kate frantically tried to scramble out of the trap.

"Get her the hell out of there!" he yelled.

"Help!" She strained again. "Help, help, help…"

"I'm coming, angel." The team circled the pit, but he couldn't wait anymore. The anguish in her voice pulled him down the steep side. He clutched thick roots and rocks to make it to the bottom, and within seconds Declan ripped her away from the wall and into his arms.

Her bloodied fingers locked on his borrowed shirt, the sobs racking her.

"I've got you." His hands shook. Declan scanned the bottom of the pit; one of the team's flashlights pointed at a mass of clothing and flesh a few feet away. The Hunter had put her in the hole with Michaels.

Turning her away from the remains, he held her until Sullivan, Anthony and Elliot pulled her from the Hunter's trap.

Anthony then hauled Declan up to the edge of the hole and pulled him from the pit.

Declan wrapped her in his arms again.

"I thought you were dead." Her voice rasped. How long had she been screaming down there? How many times had she tried to climb the walls? Had she lost hope he'd come for her?

"You can't get rid of me that easily." He needed

to get her to a hospital. The blood blooming across her shirt was still wet, sliding down her side. He'd nearly lost her, and there hadn't been a damn thing he could've done about it. Never again. She was his priority. Not recovering his memories. Not tracking down the Hunter. Kate.

"Michaels…" she said. "He was in there with me."

"You never have to worry about him again." Declan strengthened his hold on her as they trekked back the way they'd come. The ambulances would be arriving soon if they hadn't already. Intertwining his fingers with hers, he planted a kiss on the back of her hand.

As for the Hunter, Declan was only getting started.

Chapter Nine

She was going to die.

"No!" Kate shoved herself up to sit. The sudden brightness of overhead lights and incessant beeping of machinery forced panic—greedy and dark—up her still raw throat before familiar blue eyes filled her vision.

"I've got you, angel." Declan's voice triggered an automatic chain reaction within her body, urging her to relax, to trust, but the nightmare had been so real. No. Not a nightmare. A memory.

Calluses caught on her skin as he smoothed his hand down the only part of her that didn't ache. "You're safe."

"Declan." She hurt. The beeping wouldn't stop. She blinked to clear her head. She wasn't in the pit anymore. Broken pieces of memory clicked into place the longer his touch anchored her to the present, and she slipped back against the pillows of the hospital bed with his help. Her heart pounded hard behind her rib cage. "How long have I been unconscious?"

He traced the veins in the back of her hand with the pad of this thumb. A bit more color had returned to his skin, but the bruising across his face and hands stood stark against white hospital sheets. It'd been a miracle the damage hadn't been worse. Left for dead in a snare trap, stitches torn open during the fight with the man who'd shot her, but the small butterfly bandages said he'd at least seen a doctor while she'd been under anesthesia. "You got out of surgery a few hours ago. The surgeon was able to repair the damage in your shoulder, but you'll be in a sling for a few weeks."

A few hours of her life. Gone. She'd already lost so many after the surgery to remove the bullets the first time around.

Kate studied him at her bedside. He was alive. After what happened—after accepting the reality she'd never see him again—he was alive. She wasn't going to waste any more time. The brightness wouldn't lessen, but focusing on him helped the throbbing in her head.

Declan hated hospitals. Had he been by her side the entire time? "You don't have to stay here. I know how uncomfortable hospitals make you."

"I'm not going anywhere. I almost lost you, and it was worse than any trauma I've ever endured," he said.

Pressure released in her chest.

Pulling the back of her hand to his mouth, he planted a kiss on the thin, oversensitive skin. Stubble prickled against her hand, but it was the guilt in his gaze that hollowed her from the inside out. "I never should've lost track of you when you went after Michaels. I—"

"Don't." Kate moved her fingers to his mouth. He had no reason to apologize. Flashes of those terrifying seconds when she wasn't sure he'd live or die as the Hunter closed in sprinted into reality. She tried shoving it into the tiny box she'd created to survive over the last year at the back of her mind, but there were still so many unanswered questions.

Desperation burned through her. They'd almost died out there. She'd almost lost him—again— and she couldn't stand to not be touching him for another moment. Kate fisted her hand with what strength she'd managed to hold on to and pulled him into the bed.

Declan shifted closer, and she nearly collapsed into him. Settling back into the pillows, he positioned her along his side. She slipped her hand over his chest.

He pushed a strand of her hair out of her face, then framed her jaw with the palm of his hand. "I would've killed him if I hadn't found you."

"None of this is your fault. There was no way we could've known he was out there, waiting for us to spring his trap." Kate set her forehead against his and closed her eyes. His scent clung to her, spread through her system, got into her head, revitalized a part of her she believed she'd buried in his casket over a year ago. The need to be close to someone else. "The Hunter got away."

Which meant he'd be taking another victim. Their killer had shown he didn't have any sort of cooling-off period between kills. He could've already started drawing in his next prey.

"He knows those woods. He knew exactly how to vanish after stringing me up for dead. Knew where to set his traps." Declan smoothed his knuckles along her bare arms, raising goose bumps in his wake. "He had everything planned out. Even using and killing Michaels to get our attention was part of the plan."

The memories of being in that pit with Michaels's remains, of his blood on her hands, tightened the muscles down her spine. Burying her head between Declan's neck and shoulder, she counted off his heartbeat. She'd come so close to never hearing that sound again. "I tried to get out. I kept falling and the pain in my shoulder... If you hadn't pulled me out—"

"He'll never lay another hand on you." He pressed his mouth to her ear as the flood of panic rose. "You're safe now."

Safe.

Such a simple word. But for the first time in over a year, she felt it down to her bones. Because of him. Because he'd fought off death for the slightest chance of saving her life. Because he'd risked everything to ensure she'd made it out of those woods alive. With Declan, she was safe. He'd earned every ounce of trust she could give.

"There was so much blood." Kate wiped at her

face. She set her head back against his shoulder, stroking her thumb across his jaw. "How did you get out of the trap?"

"Your SOS. Blackhawk Security got the signal and responded. They cut me down, found your phone. They helped me find you." Trailing his fingertips down her back, Declan planted a kiss into her hair. "Without them, I would've died out there. You have a good team."

"They're okay." A laugh escaped her control. If she didn't have this one release, she feared she might fall apart completely. Truth was, her team was more than okay. They'd kept her going. They had her back. Declan was alive right now because of them. Kate lifted her head, studied those familiar blue eyes. "Thank you for saving my life. Again."

A smile pulled at one corner of his mouth, and her insides flipped. "That's twice now. We'll have to see what we can do to start making up the difference."

Kate studied him. Would it always be like this between them? This fire? This…need to have him close? She'd loved her husband. She'd worked hard at their marriage, but because of the things they'd dealt with in their individual careers, there'd always been a distance. Out of necessity. Otherwise the darkness of their careers would've corrupted their relationship from the inside. But now… Now she saw nothing but light. Nothing but hope.

"Are you trying to hook up with me?" she asked. "I was literally unconscious three minutes ago."

The hospital room door opened with a long slow creak.

"Look who survived a serial killer. How you doing, Doc?" Sullivan Bishop flashed a bright, straight smile before moving aside for the familiar face at his back. Hiking a thumb over his shoulder, her boss scanned the room for threats like the good SEAL he was supposed to be. "Right. This guy followed me here."

"Damn right, I did. You should've called me the minute she got out of surgery." Special Agent Ryan Dominic focused on her, then Declan, and back to her. Was that concern etched into his expression? Anger? He'd spent a good amount of time over the last year helping her through the grief, but Kate had never really been able to crack the carefully modulated control the agent kept in place.

Hands on his hips, he gave them a glimpse of that federal gun and badge he was so eager to display anytime Blackhawk Security came into the equation. "Seems not a moment too soon, either. Everyone out. I'm taking Kate into protective custody."

"Like hell you are." Declan's growl reverberated through her a split second before he stood. "The only reason she's alive is because of Blackhawk Security. You're not taking her anywhere."

She reached for him, using him for balance, and stood on shaky legs. "Ryan, I've already told you. I'm not going into hiding. You hired me to profile the Hunter, and that's exactly what I'm going to do."

"Kate, you've been through hell. I understand

that, but you are the only surviving witness in my serial case," Dominic said. "I need to know everything you remember about this guy. I need answers. Now."

She felt Declan tense beside her at the agent's tone. He dropped his hold on her, took a single step toward Dominic. "You have no idea what she's been through and pushing her to give her statement is going to do more damage than good. I don't give a damn if you need answers. She needs rest."

They didn't have time for a testosterone showdown.

"Declan, give me a minute with Special Agent Dominic." Her words were crisp. She might've survived an attack from one of the most complex killers she'd ever profiled, but she wouldn't play the victim card. She'd wasted too much of her life on that path. "You, too, Sullivan."

"I wouldn't piss her off if I were you. She's studied a lot of killers. She knows how to get rid of a body if she has to." Sullivan targeted his shoulder into Dominic's on the way to the door. "Agent Dominic."

The heat of Declan's touch ran through her as he traced the column of her spine. His gaze narrowed in on his former partner. The tendons between his neck and shoulder strained as he maneuvered toward the door. "I'll be right outside if you need me."

Kate waited until the door closed before she let the exhaustion pull her to the edge of the bed. Declan didn't need to see how weak the Hunter had made her. It would only worry him more. But with Dominic? He'd already seen her at her lowest. There wasn't much that could surprise him after what he'd helped her through.

"What are you doing, Kate?" Dropping one hand to his side, Dominic scrubbed his palm down his face with a glance out the small window next to the door. His voice lowered an octave as he studied her. "The guy comes back, and within two days you're already climbing into his lap?"

They didn't have time for this.

"Did you find her?" Kate attempted to cross her arms, but the pain in her shoulder spiraled, and she flinched before setting her arms at her side. "The other woman out there? Mary?"

Dominic sobered instantly, lowering his gaze to the floor. "Yeah, we found her. Mary Lawson. Twenty-nine. Same MO as the other three. Same similarities."

"She's one of the Hunter's." Kate sank farther onto the bed. How many more were out there in those woods? How many more would be recovered in the coming weeks? Closing her eyes, she fought back the echo of Mary's shaking voice in her head. It was time to end this.

"You're looking for a white male between the ages of thirty and thirty-five, one ninety to two hundred pounds," she said. "He knows the area and might have property nearby. It's no coincidence we recovered his first victim and Mary in the same location. Those woods are his hunting grounds. He's too intelligent to leave a paper trail, so you'll have to dig into possible aliases. The Hunter isn't leaving a whole lot of evidence behind. He's familiar with crime scenes. Could have a job or career in law enforcement or is a huge fan of true crime entertainment. Have you discovered the connection between the women aside from their appearance? Where he's finding them?"

"No." Dominic shook his head. "I have Anchorage PD canvassing around their residences so we can work up a timeline and trace their last known locations. None of the women had their phones on them when we recovered them. Unfortunately, GPS is out of the question."

He slid his hands into his pockets, his shoulders deflating on a heavy exhale, and suddenly, he looked ten years older. "Let me take you into protective custody, Kate. You need to lie low until we find this guy. The Hunter is highly organized and has been a step ahead of the FBI the entire time. He knows who you are, where you live. Hell, he probably knows the route you take to work, and your running routine. And he's not going to let you walk away."

"I won't be running anytime soon with a hole in my shoulder." She shook her head, studied the dark circles under his eyes as a weak smile thinned his mouth. This case was getting to him. Getting to them all. Dominic had been there for her when she needed him the most. He was just looking out for her now. She knew that.

"I appreciate the help, Ryan. I really do, and I trust you and the FBI to do your jobs."

Movement grabbed her attention through the blinds covering the window beside the door, and her gut said her new bodyguard had kept his promise to stick close. "I'll give you my statement, I'll answer your questions, but I'm going to make finding me as difficult for the Hunter as possible. Then we're going to nail the son of a bitch."

DECLAN SLAMMED THE driver's-side door of the SUV and rounded the hood to her side of the vehicle. It'd been three days since he'd carried her into the emergency room. Three days since he'd nearly lost her, and he couldn't get the image of her in that pit out of his damn head. Of all the memories his brain had decided to kick to the surface, it had to hold on to that one.

Gravel crunched beneath his boots as he tugged her door open. She couldn't go home. Not to the house they'd shared during their marriage and not to her apartment. Her teammate, Vincent, had offered his cabin.

Declan surveyed the surrounding woods, the lack of access now that they were out in the middle of nowhere. He could keep her safe here. Nobody—not the rest of her team, not Special Agent Dominic—knew they were out here. The Hunter would never touch her again.

"Is that a Christmas tree in the window?" Kate stepped out onto a thin veil of ice.

Snow clung to the surrounding pines and the roof

of the A-frame structure, but damn, he couldn't take his eyes off her. All that beautiful blond hair, her bright green eyes. His angel.

The cabin looked to be two stories, had a small open porch, red door and sure enough, a Christmas tree covered in white lights in the front window. Crystalized puffs formed in front of her mouth as she closed the passenger-side door behind her. "It's the middle of October. Doesn't the man believe in Halloween?"

"I doubt he's going to get many trick-or-treaters out here," he said.

"Santa's still a possibility." Kate climbed the six steps to the front porch on steady legs. The past few days in recovery had done her good. Despite the fact that she'd tried to hide it from him, he'd seen exactly how much damage the Hunter had done. How close she'd come to surrendering. But the renewed fire in her gaze revealed the bastard hadn't broken her. In fact, Declan was beginning to think nothing could.

"There is a chimney," she said.

A laugh escaped as he hauled their overnight bags from the back seat, the new stitches in his side protesting with every move. No point in thinking about any of that now. Dominic had made it clear before she'd been discharged from the hospital: Kate and her team were no longer allowed near the case. For her protection, and for theirs. Perhaps for his former partner to get all the credit, but Declan didn't know. Didn't care. He might not have access to the FBI's files anymore, but it wasn't going to stop him from finding the Hunter.

"Maybe there's cookies and milk waiting inside," he said.

She smiled at him. "There better be."

Delirium clouded his head at the sight of that perfect smile. Hell, the things she could do to him. It was no wonder his brain hadn't been able to forget her after the amnesia took root.

Locking her gaze on him, she offered him her hand. "Come on. I bet he at least has some hot chocolate to warm up."

He intertwined his fingers with hers and crossed the threshold. A wall of heat hit his skin as he set the bags in the entryway and closed the door behind them. Exposed beams ran the length of the open space, a grand stone fireplace and chimney at the long end of the living room. Furs, flannels, natural light and neutral colors welcomed them deeper into the cabin with a hint of cinnamon in the air.

"Oh, wow." She released her hold on him, pulling her green cargo jacket—the one with the hole in the sleeve—from her shoulder, and hung it on the hook near the door. She closed in on the nine-foot Christmas tree snuggled a few feet from the fireplace as glittering lights highlighted the bruise along one side of her face. She feathered her fingers over the back of one of the sofas. "If I'd known Vincent owned this place, I'd have insisted he host Blackhawk's annual Christmas party here."

"That's probably why he didn't tell you." Declan

hung his coat beside hers and keyed in the code on the panel to activate the alarm. Nobody in their right mind would come one hundred feet within this cabin, according to Vincent. The forensics expert had installed a top-of-the-line security system, and Declan intended to take advantage of it as long as they could.

He followed close on her heels. The shadows in her expression had disappeared for the time being. None of his memories—present or past—had her looking so beautiful as she did right now, illuminated in the glow of Christmas decorations. No exhaustion. No deep lines etched between her eyebrows. No darkness in her eyes. Just Kate.

"Christmas used to be my favorite holiday." She reached out for a strand of white lights, the bulb skimming down her long, delicate fingers. "When I was little, I couldn't wait for Christmas morning. My brother and I would nag my grandparents so much, they always put up the tree for me the day after Halloween. We'd spend all day hanging lights and ornaments together, listening to Christmas music and baking sugar cookies. After you and I got married and they all moved back east, you did whatever you had to to continue with the tradition. Even when you were in the middle of an important case, you always made time to indulge in my obsession."

The hollowness in his gut tightened his insides.

"I know it's stupid to get excited about a holiday with everything going on right now," she said, "but those were some of my favorite memories. Still are.

And having you back in my life, with all these decorations, it's…perfect. It's normal." Her voice was quiet. Calm. A genuine laugh escaped her lips, and the sound tightened the muscles down his spine. Green eyes glowed bright with help from the hundreds of lights on the tree, and he'd never seen a more beautiful sight.

Hell. He hadn't expected an angel to set his world on fire, yet there she stood.

"I know it's not the same," she said, "and it's fine that you don't remember—"

He couldn't keep his hands to himself any longer. Declan threaded his fingers in her hair and crushed her lips to his. Careful of her shoulder, he sandwiched her between his body and the large stone fireplace. Her light vanilla scent combined with the sharpness of cinnamon raised his awareness of her all the more.

His gut spiraled as she framed his jaw with her hand, urging him to deepen the kiss. His heart pounded hard in his chest, her sweet breaths barely audible over the throbbing of his pulse.

A shudder shook through her, and his fingers dug into her hips. Too rough. Too fast. But the need he'd tried to suppress had clawed to the surface the second he'd found her in that damn pit. He'd thought far too much about what could've happened if he hadn't followed the training ingrained in his head. He could've lost her. She could've died. And he would have never forgiven himself.

She pulled back, her shoulders rising on a strong inhale, but it was the return of the shadows in her eyes that sent ice through him. Fingers pressed against her lips, she slumped against the stone wall behind her. "I can't do this."

"I hurt you," he said.

Not a question. Kate Monroe was the strongest, most intelligent woman he'd ever met, but even a woman who dealt in death by getting into the minds of killers had her limits. She'd been through more the past four days—hell, the past year—than he could ever know, and he'd put his own selfish need ahead of her own.

"No. It's not you." She shook her head, rolling her lips between her teeth. She pushed her uninjured hand through her hair as tears welled, and his heart sank. A humorless laugh bubbled past her kiss-stung lips. "I... I close my eyes, and I'm right back in the bottom of that pit."

Hell. His hand slipped down her arm. He should've killed the SOB when he had the chance, should've been more prepared, put her safety first.

Her scent worked deep into his lungs, clearing his head. None of that mattered right now. This, right here. This mattered. And he'd do anything to chase the nightmares away. "How can I help?"

"Will you hold me? No expectations. No strings. No questions," she said.

The tears fell freely now, and he feathered the pad of this thumb across her cheek.

Another shake of her head. "I know I said I was fine at the hospital, but I'm not fine, Declan. I've showered, changed my clothes, I've washed the blood off my skin, but I still feel him. I'm not strong enough to do this. I thought I was, but I was wrong."

"Come here." Declan wrapped her in his arms, and she set her head against him. Right where she belonged. With a quick glance, he ensured he'd set the alarm, then positioned his arm beneath her knees. In a quick maneuver that pulled at the fresh stitches in his side, he hauled her into his arms and walked around the sofa. He'd endure a thousand ripped stitches if it meant he got to hold her like this.

He set her gently on the fur rug in front of the fireplace, taking position at her back, his arm wrapped around her midsection. He smoothed back the stray hairs around her ear and planted a kiss at the tendon between her neck and shoulder. "I'll hold you as long as you need, angel."

Stiffness slowly drained from her, and within minutes her breathing evened. Inhale. Exhale.

He didn't know how long they lay there as he counted her breaths, but night had started falling again, and he realized she'd drifted to sleep in his arms. Flames crackled in the stone hearth, shifting the shadows across her features. Exhaustion and her sweet scent pulled him closer to oblivion, to the point he couldn't fight it anymore. The echo of her scream in the woods cut through him as sleep closed in but he only held her tighter.

She was alive. She was safe. The truth settled deep into Declan's bones as he slipped into unconsciousness. She was his.

Chapter Ten

Kate shifted onto her side, hundreds of lit Christmas lights sparkling above her. A smile pulled at one corner of her mouth at the sight as she stretched her aching muscles. When was the last time she'd slept so well? Months? A year? The past four days had taken a toll, but for the first time since dodging bullets back at the house, she felt almost human. What had changed?

She raised her head at a hard thumping noise from outside, and she straightened. Rubbing her fingers across one eye, she pushed to her feet. She already knew the answer. "Declan?"

A tray with a steaming mug of hot chocolate and a slip of paper sat on the sofa cushion near the fur rug they'd fallen asleep on. She breathed in the combination of cinnamon and cocoa. How did he know she liked to sprinkle cinnamon on top of her hot chocolate? She pinched the piece of paper between two fingers.

Take your time and dress warm before you meet me outside.

Replacing the note, she picked up the mug. Heat spread through her as she sipped and chased back the chill that had settled there since she'd been tossed into the pit. Her shoulder ached, but it was nothing compared to recovering from three bullet wounds and the handful of surgeries afterward. Her favorite hot beverage helped. The IOU list she'd created in her head for Declan had already started growing out of control.

She changed into warmer clothes—harder than anticipated with a hole in her shoulder—and slid on her boots before stepping onto the front porch. The light veil of snow coating everything heralded the arrival of winter. She scanned the front yard for the source of the rhythmic sound, but there was no sign of Declan. Following the stone path around to the back of the cabin, she tamped down the need to search the trees at every movement, every sound.

She was safe here. She had to believe that. Otherwise…

Circling around the back of the cabin, Kate slowed as Declan came into sight.

He'd shed his jacket, and thick bands of muscle tightened and released down his back, across his shoulders, in his arms. Despite the cold, sweat formed a thin layer across his brow as he heaped a shovelful of snow onto a pile next to the in-ground firepit.

The longer she studied him, the more the knot in her gut eased. "I'm pretty sure Vincent doesn't expect you to shovel snow while we're here."

Declan spun, and that smile of his hiked her blood pressure higher as he balanced one hand on the snow shovel. "Good morning." Gleaming blue eyes focused on her, and the world disappeared. "I was about to come dump a handful of snow on you to wake you up."

"Is that what all this is for?" Warmth climbed up her neck and into her face as snow fell around them. He made her feel warm, safe, cared for. Then again, he'd had that skill from the moment he'd inserted himself back into her life. When he'd died, she'd felt as though she'd shattered into a million pieces, and it had taken close to a year to be able to put herself back together.

But for the first time in a long time, the pieces fit. She was starting to feel whole, to think of a future outside of grieving, outside of hunting down killers. A future with Declan. And last night, she could've sworn she fit perfectly against him.

Kate walked up to the firepit. Boxes of graham crackers, bags of marshmallows and packages of chocolate bars sat a few feet away. S'mores? "Quite the breakfast you have planned."

"You only live once. Well, not in my case, but you get the point." Flakes collected in his hair as he closed the short distance between them. For an instant, she could've sworn his pupils darkened as he studied the sling around her arm. "How's the pain?"

"Better today." She didn't want to think about the hole in her shoulder, how it got there, who'd shot her or why. She wanted the world to stop, wanted to close her eyes and for once not see herself at the bottom of that pit with Brian Michaels's remains. She wanted her life back. But the Hunter had made that impossible. No matter how many times she tried to convince herself otherwise, the man who'd trapped her wasn't finished. The world wouldn't stop just because she needed it to.

He wasn't done killing, and he wasn't finished with her.

Kate clenched her fists to hold on to a bit of warmth and forced a smile. "Did you build a snow fort?"

"Yeah. Still needs some finishing touches, but I thought it'd be fun to get some sunshine, start a fire and relive all those favorite Christmas memories of yours." Declan narrowed his eyes at her, then he hefted the shovel from the ground and faced the mound of snow he'd built. "What do you say, Monroe? Ready to make yourself sick from eating too much chocolate?"

He'd done this for her?

Kate reached to frame his jaw with her hand. His stubble scraped along her palms, and he closed his eyes as though he were committing the moment to memory. Hope built inside her, and she planted a soft kiss against his cheek. Her heart skipped a beat as a flood of need overwhelmed her reluctance. She leaned in a second time, kissing the corner of his mouth. "Thank you. For all of this. For saving my life. For…everything."

"Be careful, Kate." His gaze was on her again,

filled with molten heat. Declan trailed his free hand to her hips beneath the hem of her jacket, holding her in place. "I only have so much control when it comes to you."

"If there's one thing I've learned over the past few days, it's that you won't hurt me. I trust you." She swiped her tongue across her bottom lip, and his gaze shot to her mouth.

The past four days—the past year of her life— had been filled with nothing but fear, pain and death. She couldn't live like that anymore. Not when the man standing in front of her made her feel so much more.

Fisting her hand in his shirt collar, she pulled him into her. With her heart racing so fast and hard, she feared he might hear the chaotic beat, but she knew exactly what she was asking in that moment. A chance to forget. A chance to move on. They'd escape the pain for a bit, then she'd wake up tomorrow, and reality would come screaming back.

"Control is the last thing I want right now," she said.

Then he was the one to kiss her. He swept inside her mouth without hesitation, and she committed every ounce of her being to him in that moment. No turning back. No letting the past interject between them anymore. The Declan Monroe she'd married had died that night in their home after a fatal shooting. She'd always love him—always have memories of him—but right now, she had a second chance.

And she was going to take it.

Snowflakes burned against her exposed skin as he deepened the kiss. He discarded the shovel and his hold strengthened around her back, molding her against him. The shooting, Michaels's involvement with the Hunter, the nightmares, it all vanished as Declan's fingers pressed into her spine.

"We almost died out there, and those were the most terrifying hours of my life. I thought I was going to lose you all over again." She brushed her fingertips down his throat, over his Adam's apple. "I don't want to waste another minute being afraid, Declan."

He trailed his fingers along the back of her arm, every inch prompting new desire. Lacing his fingers with hers, he tugged her to the entrance of the snow fort he'd built. "You never have to be afraid with me at your side. I'll take a hundred more bullets, hang upside down for eternity and fight for you until my last breath if it means I get to be with you. I'm not going anywhere."

He picked up the bag of s'mores ingredients. Pulling her inside the snow fort, Declan rolled onto his back, on top of layers of blankets he'd laid out, and she did the same. "What do you think? Just like your childhood?"

"Not exactly. I wasn't allowed to have boys inside my fort as a kid." Gleaming ice surrounded them, but nothing but warmth penetrated through her clothing as she shifted beside him. "I'm thinking after the past few days we've had, we can break another rule while we're at it and have s'mores for breakfast."

"Coming right up." Declan made quick work of starting the fire in the pit outside their snow cave door as she unpackaged the ingredients. He slid back inside, claiming his roasting stick and an oversize marshmallow. Within a minute, the marshmallows were perfectly brown, the scent of fire and pure sugar in the air as they assembled their treats.

He bit into the mess, leaving a bit of marshmallow and chocolate on his chin. "All right. You've got sugar for breakfast and a guy in your snow fort. What other rules are you interested in breaking today?"

"Just one more." Reaching out, she skimmed her thumb over his bottom lip to wipe away the remnants of their sugar rush. Piercing blue eyes focused on her, and every cell in her body fizzed with awareness. Sunlight bore down on the fort, droplets of freezing water pooling at the edges of the blankets. A chunk of ice landed at her feet, but she wasn't going to rush this. "But with the fort coming down around us, I recommend we make this first time fast."

Kate set her chocolate-and-marshmallow breakfast aside and reached for her jacket. Sliding her one arm out, she tossed it aside and went for the Velcro on her sling. No more stalling. No more living in the past. The future sat right in front of her, waiting for her to make a choice she never thought she'd have to make. And she'd made it.

She planted her hand over his sternum. "Screw the rules."

Declan threaded his fingers in her hair, then shifted her onto her back as he flashed that brilliant smile. "I was never a fan of them anyway."

DECLAN SLIPPED FROM the king-size sheets they'd spent the rest of day underneath and grabbed his clothes before stalking toward the door. No more mistakes. He'd let that bastard get his hands on her once. He wouldn't let it happen again. He wasn't about to let her go, and he'd do whatever it took to protect her.

Even if it meant lying to her a bit longer.

Because once she discovered the truth, discovered he wasn't the man she thought him to be, she wouldn't want him anymore.

Oranges, yellows and reds bled through the cabin's windows as the sun set in the west. He dressed quickly, then extracted her laptop from her bag beside the door. Taking position on one of the bar stools at the granite countertop, he dimmed the screen and typed the online access address for the FBI into the browser. The window changed, demanding a login and password. That bit of memory had come to the surface while he dug out the snow fort, and he typed in Special Agent Declan Monroe's credentials.

Access granted.

Kate's teammate, Elizabeth, had been assigned to review his old case files for the BAU, but she wasn't an agent. She didn't hunt the monsters in the dark. He did, and there had to be something he could work with—a clue, anything in these old files—he could follow to nail the perp with one of his own damn arrows. Somehow, the Hunter knew him, and Declan would make him pay for dragging Kate into his sick game.

He read through countless case files, one after the other. Crime scene photos, witness statements, arrest reports. Nothing jogged his memory, none of it linked to any other cases where an arrow was part of the killer's MO. He had...nothing.

Declan rubbed at his eyes as frustration burrowed deeper. A single file on Kate's desktop peeked out from behind the window he'd been working in. Case 306-AK-4442. The FBI's internal offense code 306 categorized the file under serial killings, AK assigned the file to the Bureau's Alaskan field office and the last number was unique to the case. The Hunter's case.

Double tapping on the file folder, he scanned the evidence from the Hunter's latest trophy, the woman Kate had found in the field. Kate and Declan might've been banned from working the case officially, but the FBI hadn't ordered her to delete her case files. An oversight on Dominic's part, but Declan wasn't above taking advantage. Not when Kate's life was in danger.

Mary Lawson. She fit the unsub's MO, making her the perfect prey. But what were the chances the killer had found not two but four single women close to their thirties with blond hair and green eyes in this city? What was the connection? His rage boiled hot inside of him, a blistering fury that demanded he end the son of a bitch. "When are you going to try for her again, you bastard?"

The kitchen lights brightened, and his spine went rock hard as he closed down the file window.

"You want to go after him alone." She moved into his peripheral vision, her fingers trailing across his shoulders, and his grip on the counter relaxed. She took a seat beside him, her voice devoid of emotion. No plea to get him to stop. No disappointment in his decision. Nothing. "Even though we're off the case, you can't let the Hunter get away with what he did."

"He tried to kill you." But he couldn't think about that right now. He had to focus on the evidence, had to find a lead. Because the Hunter wasn't finished. He'd come after Kate again. He'd try to take her away. That wasn't happening. "And for all you know, I could be researching different s'more recipes."

"Okay, first, you're a horrible liar," she said.

If only that were true.

"Second, I know you, Declan." She reached across the laptop and hit a command to bring up the Hunter's files. He inwardly flinched. "You might not have all your memories, but some things are ingrained too deep. Doubling down on a case is something you used to do as an agent, even when you only had a hunch. Third, there's no other way to make s'mores. I don't care what the internet says."

Her green gaze glowed from the laptop's brightness. She pulled her hand away as she stood. "Besides, I'm not sure he was trying to kill us. There were faster ways to accomplish the task, and he wouldn't have worn a mask or disguised his voice if that was his intention."

"What then? He's dressing up for Halloween?" he asked.

"I think he was testing us." Her thin robe fluttered around her knees as she moved to the refrigerator. She pulled a carton of eggs and a gallon of milk from the fridge and set them on the island in front of him. "He killed Michaels and broke his own MO. He's not operating out of some undeniable urge to kill like most serials. The Hunter wanted us— wanted *me*—to see what he's capable of. Maybe to prove he's above my skills as a profiler, which is certainly looking to be true for the time being."

Declan stood, coming around the countertop. "We're going to catch this guy, Kate." They had to. Otherwise… He shut down that line of thought. No. He wouldn't think about that. He wouldn't think about losing her like that.

"I let my personal problems get in the way of doing my job. Again." She twisted the cap off the milk and selected a brightly colored ceramic mixing bowl from the cabinet. She cracked one egg into the bowl, then another. "How exactly are we supposed to catch him when I can't even wrap my head around the fact you're standing in this kitchen with me?"

"You need to know, there was nothing you could've done for Michaels," he said. "He didn't become one of your patients by chance. He was placed in your path. Someone sent him to shoot you."

Her mouth dropped open, and she stumbled away from the counter. The egg in her hand fell to the floor, but she didn't move to clean it up. Eyes wide, she licked her lips. "What did you say?"

"Right before I heard those gunshots in the woods, I found Michaels." Declan lowered his voice.

It'd all been in his statement to the Anchorage PD and FBI while she was in surgery, but Kate had been removed from the case right afterward. She had no reason to believe she still had access to those files. No reason to go back and read his statement. If anything, she'd probably made the effort to avoid anything to do with the case since being pulled from that damn hole in the ground.

"His throat had been cut, but before he died, he told me he was hired to fire those shots. Someone paid him to pull the trigger a year ago and again the other day. He was a pawn, Kate. You did nothing wrong."

"You think that person who hired him is the Hunter." She worked to swallow, her gaze distant as she studied the broken egg on the floor. Her fingers went to the scar at the collar of her T-shirt, a nervous habit that had increased over the last few days.

"I guess that explains why both Michaels and our serial killer were in those woods at the same time, but that still doesn't make sense. The Hunter is the one with the fascination for blonde women with green eyes. Not Michaels." She looked up at him. "Why would he send one of my patients after me at all? And with a gun? Serial killing teams are rare, but if they were partners, wouldn't they have the same MO? They build off each other, they work hard—together—to distort the evidence and confuse law enforcement. Studies have shown they have a smaller chance of getting caught that way because police think they're only after one unsub instead of two distinct killers."

He'd given it a lot of thought since walking out of those woods with her in his arms and again as he'd traced the scar tissue across her chest while she slept. There was only one explanation. Declan rested his hip against the counter, folding his arms across as his own scars burned with awareness. "I don't think the bullets were meant for you."

She lowered her hand. "There was only one other person in that house, which means—"

"Michaels was sent to kill me." The bastard had almost succeeded. Twice. Only, Kate had gotten caught in the cross fire. Was that why the Hunter cut Michaels's throat? Had it been punishment for his partner nearly killing the target he was really after?

The feel of the cold granite kept the rage at bay. For now. Because Kate had been right. Declan wanted to go after him. The Hunter had started this battle, but Declan would bring the war. "I was there, Kate. Both times. That can't be a coincidence."

"If the Hunter wanted you out of the way to get to me, why wait over a year to try again?" she asked. "Why target those four other women when he had so many opportunities to take me?"

"Maybe he couldn't get to you, even with me out of the picture." Blackhawk Security watched their own and had an entire arsenal at their disposal. Their killer wouldn't want that kind of attention or heat.

Declan ran a hand through his hair, focusing on the bowl of milk and egg she'd left on the counter. "Or it's like you said in your profile. He wants us to see his work, rub it in our faces that we haven't stopped him before now. Punishing us." Air rushed from his lungs as the realization hit. Damn it. He should've seen it before. He should've known. "Punishing you. Because he can't bring himself to hurt you."

"You're saying I'm the focus of his kills." Color drained from her face, her rough exhale loud in his ears. Profilers didn't catch killers. She gave the men and women who did the details to accomplish their task. Being the target of a psychopath had never been part of the job description.

Kate straightened. "Those women are being hunted in the middle of the woods—dying with arrows through their hearts—because of me? Is that what you're saying?"

Declan wrapped his hands around her arms, careful of the bullet graze on one side. The lit Christmas lights deepened the shadows in her eyes, an opposite effect of the night before, and everything inside of him went cold. The Hunter had put those shadows there, and Declan would make damn sure he paid for it. "This is not your fault, Kate. Don't you dare let him get to you this way. The shooting, those women's deaths, what happened to me, none of it is on you."

"I know all that." Her words cut through him. "But this killer… He's not like anything I've encountered before, and he's good at what he does. He's gotten in my head, and I can't get him out, okay?"

Nothing but strength and determination showed in her expression, and damn if that wasn't the sexiest thing he'd ever seen. Kate Monroe had been through hell and back, but the locking of her jaw said she wouldn't be playing the part of victim anytime soon.

"You don't have to worry about my guilt," she said. "If anyone should be worried, it's him. I'm not going to let him get away with this." Kate collected a handful of paper towels and scooped the broken egg off the floor. Throwing it in the trash, she set back to work on the ingredients for their dinner. "He thinks he's better at hunting than I am, but I'm going to show him he's wrong."

Chapter Eleven

"If we accept our theory that I'm his ultimate prey, then the killer thinks he knows me. But I think finding a connection between the women needs to be the priority," Kate said.

Because there had to be one beyond just a similarity to her looks. Kate might've been the Hunter's ultimate target according to their theory, but she didn't know any of the victims. As far as she could tell, she'd never met them before. Not working as a psychologist and not for Blackhawk Security. It was too easy to assume their killer had found them on the street. So how was the Hunter coming into contact with them?

"However small," she said. "It'll tell us how he's choosing his victims and help us stop the next abduction. You and I both know he isn't finished. If anything, I believe he's just getting started."

"You read my mind." Declan spun the laptop toward her, the mess of French toast forgotten on the counter as four young faces stared back at her from the screen. "Brittney Sutherland, Holly Belcher, Carrie Fleming and Mary Lawson."

"Wait, why does that second name sound familiar?" Kate shifted closer to the screen as instinct flared. She'd read that name before and not in the files Dominic had given her when he'd brought her onto the case. It hadn't clicked until now. "Holly Belcher."

"I thought the same thing when I brought up her file. Turns out her brother went missing last year. She was all over the news." Declan scrolled through the digital file. "She and her mother were pleading with anyone who had information about his disappearance to call Anchorage PD over every news channel who'd give them air time."

A missing person case.

"I can only imagine what that mother is going through right now," Kate said. "First her son, then her daughter."

Losing Declan had been one thing. Losing two children within the span of a year? Kate swallowed as her throat swelled. Then again, she'd lost a child, too, hadn't she? She hadn't gotten to meet the tiny life that had been growing inside of her, but a life had been ripped from her all the same. Her gaze slid to Declan, across his shoulders, down his spine, and it took everything in her not to imagine what that life might look like today.

"Did they ever find him?" she asked. "The son?"

"No. No sign of him according to the FBI's report. He was finally presumed dead a few months ago by the lead investigating agent." Declan shook his head, leaning back on the bar stool as he crossed his arms over his muscled chest.

Kate eased away from the screen. "Now his sister is a serial killer's trophy."

Didn't seem fair after everything the family had already been through. Her heart broke a fraction more as she straightened. But she could still get them justice. She could stop the Hunter from taking more women.

"Michaels was a former patient," Declan said. "There's a chance the Hunter is, too."

"It's possible, but even if we knew his identity, we won't be able to get those files from their current doctors without a judge," she said. "If we were granted a warrant, any leads we get from them won't be usable in court. I'm not a practicing psychologist anymore, but doctor-patient confidentiality is still in effect."

The Hunter was one of the most complicated killers she'd studied. He was organized, intelligent and controlled. If he'd been seeing a psychologist, it would be impossible to pick him out of a stack of files due to his ability to blend in, to lie. To make everyone around him believe he was just like them.

Kate rolled her bottom lip into her mouth and bit down to keep herself in the moment. There had to be something they could use. Every victim had unknowingly attracted the Hunter in some way, brought him into their lives.

"What if he targeted Holly because of her media

appearances?" she asked. "Were any of the other women in the spotlight? The more we learn about the victims, the more we'll learn about their killer."

Declan's fingers flew over the keyboard, the screen switching from the second victim to the first. The Hunter had started with Brittney Sutherland, as far as the authorities knew. She'd been the first victim recovered, but there was a chance there were others out there. "You're not going to believe this."

"What?" Kate forced herself to look past the photo of the victim and read the FBI's report. Her heart jerked in her chest as she read through the lead agent's notes. "Is that…"

"Another missing person report," he said. "Only this is for the first victim's mother."

"Two victims, both tied to separate missing persons cases?" That was too much of a coincidence. What were the chances two of the Hunter's victims had loved ones missing within in the same time frame? "Check the others. Carrie Fleming and Mary Lawson."

The screen changed as he pulled the next two files. "Carrie was brought in for questioning when her best friend disappeared from a bar a few months ago, and Mary's roommate went missing last week."

"That's how he's finding them." She tapped the screen. Her arm brushed against Declan's, and her entire body caught fire with adrenaline. They had a lead. "The crime scenes where each victim was left are too complex, too clean. I'd originally thought he was a true crime buff, maybe studied a bit of forensics, but this points to law enforcement. Someone in the FBI is targeting women who've been brought in for questioning during missing persons investigations. It's the perfect cover."

"The FBI has dozens of agents assigned to their missing persons task force, Kate. We know the Hunter is local to Anchorage, knows the area and is a big-time hunter, but the Bureau won't ever give us access to the personnel files without a warrant. Even then, by the time we get through the files, another woman could go missing." Declan smoothed his hand over his wound. "I have your back, but we'll have to come at this another way."

Heat worked through her. She had his back, too, and in that moment, she trusted him more than she'd ever trusted anyone since his death. Over the last year, she'd fought to keep her head above water, fought for her team, fought with everything she had not to dissolve into nothingness, but with him here, it was easier. There was a light at the end of the tunnel.

"Our unsub had to be assigned to all four of our victims' cases to come into contact with them, right? He didn't choose these women at random. He got close to them during the investigations, probably talked with them a few times. Became familiar with their lives." She blinked to clear the exhaustion from her head. They'd been running on fumes and fear for the last few days. Barely eaten more than marshmallows and chocolate. Barely slept. But she wouldn't stop. Not until they identified the Hunter and brought his victims and their families justice. "Who was the lead agent?"

Scanning the reports, Declan confirmed a commonality. "Special Agent Kenneth Winter headed all four missing persons cases, but these are career-making cases. A lot of agents and officers wanted in. The chief of police included. Wait. I've heard that name before."

Her stomach sank. "He's Dominic's partner." The BAU's newest agent had always been desperate to prove himself on the hardest cases. If he was responsible for these women's deaths, what was harder than making it look like some other perpetrator had delivered the killing shot while taking credit for the collar in the end? Winter was over six feet tall, close to one hundred and ninety pounds. Had he been the one to toss her in that pit to die?

Kate cleared her throat, shook her head to dislodge the memory. Like Declan said, these were career-making cases. Winter might be one name out of dozens all assigned to work missing persons cases. They'd have to dig deeper into each case.

"Blackhawk Security has a contact in Anchorage PD. Maybe she can give us some insight into who might've taken a special interest in the women during the investigations." Kate refocused on the dinner mess on the kitchen counter. Her body ached from tension, from being shot with an arrow, from the last four days. She grew heavy as a wave of dizziness took hold. "I'll let Dominic know he might want to take a closer look at the missing persons cases."

And his partner.

"Kate, you're bottoming out." Declan pushed away from the laptop and caged her against the cool countertop. "You need to get something other than sugar in you, shower and sleep for at least few hours. You're no good to any of those women if you're dead on your feet. I'll fill Dominic in and finish up the mess here."

"Thank you." She gripped the granite. He was right. Of course he was. If she didn't take a step back now, the Hunter would only take advantage of her weakness. But the thought of stepping away— even after Dominic had ordered her to cut ties to the case, even for a few hours—pooled dread at the base of her spine.

The Hunter had made this personal. He'd recruited Michaels to do his dirty work. Twice. He'd taken her husband's memories, taken her unborn baby, taken everything that mattered. The killer was still out there, and he wouldn't wait around for her to get herself together. He'd strike when she least expected it.

"For everything," she said. "Truth is, I feel better when I'm with you." Not scared. Not weak. Kate framed Declan's face with her uninjured hand, his five-o'clock shadow bristling against her palm. She didn't have to hide from him. No secrets. No lies. No pretending. He'd pulled her from the darkness and out into the light, given her a second chance.

He'd saved her, and she trusted him straight to her core. He would catch her long before she ever fell. She'd fight like hell to keep him at her side.

"I've hunted at least a dozen monsters between my job at Blackhawk Security and consulting for the FBI, but this one…" Dropping her hand, she took a deep, cleansing breath and shook her head. "I'm glad you're here. I wouldn't want to work this case without you."

"Me, too. If for no other reason than having my own personal partner with benefits," he said. "Pretty sure Dominic and I never had that kind of relationship."

Kate pressed her lower back into the counter. Was this a relationship? Sure, they'd slept together in that perfect little snow fort he'd built out back, but it had started simply as a way to stop the nightmares, to distract her from the harsh reality crashing down around them both. Only, being with Declan had become so much more. Hadn't it?

He leaned into her, his mouth mere centimeters from hers. His exhale brushed against the thin skin of her collarbone as he studied her from forehead to chin. Sliding his hand to her wrist, he traced the oversensitive veins running up her arm. "Now stop stalling and get in the shower. Because, angel, you smell awful."

A burst of laughter escaped her lips, and she tipped her head up toward the ceiling. "Trust me when I say this, I don't smell as bad as you do." Desire pushed through her as she grabbed his shirt collar and tugged him back toward the bedroom. "But it's a good thing I have a solution for that."

DAWN BROKE THROUGH the trees, but the feel of a new day hadn't struck yet. With Kate asleep in his arms, it was easy to imagine the nightmares didn't wait outside these walls. They could lie here, waste the day away in bed, surviving off nothing but each other's body heat and whatever they could find in the pantry. But the world wouldn't stop for them and neither would the Hunter.

"I can almost see the wheels spinning in your head." Her fingers smoothed between his eyebrows. Kate pulled the sheets around her, hiking her uninjured hand beneath her head. Mesmerizing green eyes followed the path of her fingers as she reached out to trace one of his scars. "Trying to figure out how to sneak out of here without waking me up again? It won't work."

"Quite the opposite. I was devising a plan to convince you to stay in bed all day long." Taking her chin between his thumb and first finger, he rolled into her. He needed to tell her the truth. He'd become the one person in this world she could rely on, and he intended to keep it that way. Hell, he was a jerk for keeping her in the dark this long.

Her soft moan vibrated against him as she closed her eyes. "Wouldn't take too much convincing, but since you've already gone through all that trouble, I'll let you plead your case."

He pulled her flush against him with his arm. His

mouth crashed onto hers, and Declan pushed everything he had into that kiss. The loneliness of waking up in that hospital room alone, the pain from the bullet wound in his side, the fear of losing her all over again. She shouldered it all and expected nothing in return. That was the kind of woman she was. Considerate, caring, honest.

Everything he wasn't.

"I'm beginning to see your point, but I think I need to hear a bit more of your defense." She smiled against his mouth, then skimmed her fingertips along his bottom lip. Setting her ear over his heart, she ran one hand through her hair. "It's also time we got on the same page. I know I said after this investigation was over it'd be better if we go our separate ways, but a lot has happened since then."

Anxiety clawed through him. "Kate, wait—"

"Please just let me finish before I lose my nerve." Straightening, she placed a hand over the gauze taped to her shoulder. "For the past year I've been lost. I've helped dozens of patients move past their trauma in my career, but for the longest time, I couldn't take my own damn advice. When it came right down to it, we were together for so long, I'd forgotten how to be alone."

She shook her head. "I hated it. I was cold inside. I'd given up hope of ever finding another person who could make me feel the way you did. I threw myself into my work because helping my clients was the only thing that made me feel alive. Until you walked back into that house five days ago."

Kate hiked the sheets farther up her body. "When you kiss me, I see a light at the end of this dark, lonely tunnel I've been stuck inside. You're the strongest, most selfless man I've ever known, and I don't want to give that up. I don't want to give you up." She smoothed her hand over his chest. "I want you to stay. I want us to try to make sense of whatever's happening between us. It won't be easy, but I think it'll be worth it." She placed her hand over his sternum. "So that's how I feel. Now you tell me how you feel."

Heat worked through him, and he fisted his hands in the sheets. Committing the past few minutes to memory, Declan filled his lungs with her sweet vanilla scent. He had to tell her the truth, pray she'd still want him despite the lie. And if she didn't... His gut tightened. Things would have to go back to the way they were. He'd rebuild his life. Without her. "Kate, there's something you need to know before we—"

A soft ringing reached his ears, and she lowered her forehead onto his chest. Her hair tickled his overheated skin as she pushed away to reach for her phone on the nightstand. "Hold that thought." Bringing it to her ear, she pegged him with a smile, and his blood pressure spiked. "Kate Monroe."

The smile disappeared, her gaze sinking into the sheets. Her tongue swiped across her bottom lip, and she pushed herself upright. She threw her legs over the side of the bed and positioned the phone between her neck and shoulder as she reached for her discarded clothing on the floor. "When?"

Everything inside of him shut down.

"Okay." Kate hauled her T-shirt over her head, careful of her wound. Slipping into her jeans, she hopped to pull them around her waist, and Declan shoved out of the bed. "I'll be right there."

She tossed the phone onto the bed, turning away from him.

"Kate?" Concern deepened his voice and ignited his instincts with battle-ready precision. "Tell me who was on the phone."

"That was Ryan. Sorry, Special Agent Dominic." She turned, biting down on her thumbnail. "He got our message about the connection between the women and started digging into any active missing persons cases the FBI is investigating." Kate ran a hand through her hair. She did that when she tried to hide the emotions fighting for release inside, but she couldn't hide from him. The tension along her spine gave her away, and he rounded the bed in order to close the distance between them. "He believes another woman has been taken. And that his partner is responsible."

"Kenneth Winter. But what makes you think Dominic isn't involved? That him pulling you back in isn't some kind of trap? They're partners. They're assigned the same cases." As far as Declan knew, Anchorage PD and the FBI were still analyzing the last scene, and the Hunter had already taken another victim? Damn it. They couldn't keep up with this guy.

"Serial killing teams are rare, but even so, Dominic's name isn't on any of the missing person reports." Kate shook her head. "I know Ryan. He bleeds red, white and blue for the FBI."

"So Dominic wants to keep this quiet until he has enough evidence to bring his partner in for questioning," Declan said. "That's why he called you back in?"

"He wants as many available eyes on this case as he can get. He's at a scene he believes is the last known location of a missing woman who fits the Hunter's MO." She reached for her green cargo jacket and slipped into her boots. "There's no rhyme or reason to this unsub's attacks, and it's only going to get worse from here. We need to catch this guy. If there's a chance this latest victim can be brought home before we find her with an arrow through the heart, Dominic is going to take the risk of losing his job to do it." Straightening, she softened her expression. "He's going to email me the details in a few minutes, but I really want to finish our conversation."

"This case has to take priority." Dominic's call had bought Declan some time. He'd tell her the truth soon, but right now, bringing down the unsub who'd set this all in motion had to come first. "Don't worry. We have time. We'll do what we have to do to get those families justice, then talk about us."

"So there's an us?" Her eyes glittered as sunlight speared through the windows. She stepped toward him, slipped her arms around his waist and stared up at him.

"I've waited a long time to find the woman in my dreams. Do you think I'm going to walk away after everything we've been through?" Twisting a strand of her hand around his finger, he set his forehead against hers. He tilted her chin higher and planted a soft kiss on her mouth. "You accept my past, support me in the present and have given me a glimpse of my future. You're my armor, and you and I will always be unfinished business."

That angelic smile of hers overwhelmed her expression, and he couldn't help but smile back. "Not sure I had a choice in those first two things," she said. "Finding out your husband isn't dead after all is kind of a sink-or-swim situation."

"Good thing your personnel file says you're scuba certified, then." His laugh rumbled through him, and for the first time he could remember, the gutting hollowness inside didn't ache. "Maybe after all this is over, you can show off some of those skills on a beach far the hell away from here."

She wrapped her arms around his neck, hiking herself onto her tiptoes. "Hot sand, cold drinks and nothing but the ocean and room service? I could get on board with that."

He nibbled at her bottom lip, sliding his arms around her waist. Kissing a trail down her neck, he locked on their reflection in a standalone mirror against the wall. This. This was what he wanted.

Her, for the rest of his life. Every wound he'd incurred, every scar left behind, they all paved the way to this moment, to her. Declan would fight until his last breath to protect her.

Her tablet pinged with an incoming message, and she turned in his arms at the sound. "That's probably the details Dominic said he'd send over. Don't go anywhere."

"Wouldn't dream of it," he said.

Kate unwrapped her arms and crossed back to the nightstand beside the bed. He watched as she tapped the screen, confusion deepening the distinctive lines between her eyebrows. "That's not… right."

"What is it?" He pushed his feet into his boots, the mattress dipping under his weight as he bent to tie them. His gut sank. Had law enforcement been too late? Declan pushed upright, took a single step forward. "Did they already find her?"

"No." She snapped her attention up and tossed the device face up onto the bed.

Every muscle down his spine tightened as he studied the screen. Surveillance photos taken from outside her apartment—of Declan—dated a few weeks ago.

"Looks like we're going to have to hold off on that beach vacation," she said.

Chapter Twelve

"How did you know I like cinnamon in my hot chocolate?" The dates on those surveillance photos couldn't be right. If they were... Then Declan had been lying to her all this time.

Nausea churned in her gut. Lying about his memories. Lying about not knowing who she was. The photos of him watching her apartment and their home two weeks ago proved that.

"That's not the question you want to ask, Kate." He straightened from tying his boots, gripping the edge of the mattress, his attention on her tablet. "Ask me."

She swallowed around the bile rising up her throat. The truth dried out her mouth and pulled at her body until her knees weakened. It took everything to keep herself upright, but the air had been taken right out of her. Her scars burned as though she'd been shot all over again. Pain spread from her shoulder down through the rest of her arm. Or was it the scars in her heart tearing open again?

"How long have you had your memories back?" she asked.

"Hard to say." Piercing blue eyes locked on her, and the room spun. Was that an admission? Veins struggled to break through the skin of his forearms the harder his fingers clenched the edge of the mattress. "They still come in bits and pieces. I don't remember everything."

"But you knew who I was before you walked into our house that night, right? You knew I was your wife, and you stayed away anyway. You let me think you were still dead." Her eyes burned as betrayal hit.

Kate forced herself to take a deep breath to drown the nausea, but his clean, masculine scent filled her system instead. The grief, the pain he'd helped ebb clawed through her, deepening the fissures Brian Michaels had put there in the first place. A combination of sorrow and rage exploded inside her. Hot tears burned a path down her face. Apparently, Declan had only come back into her life to finish the job.

"Why didn't you tell me the truth? Why keep me in the dark? I could've helped you sooner," she said.

He stood, towering over her to the point she had to crane her head back to look at him. "I woke up with four bullet wounds, Kate. I had no memory of how they'd gotten there or who pulled the trigger. For all I knew, you were the reason I was in that hospital bed." He gripped his fists at his side. "I wasn't sure I could trust you. I thought if I inserted myself back into your life pretending not to know anything about you, you could help me regain the rest of my memories and get me access to my personnel file with the FBI. Which you have."

"You used me." Plain and simple. He'd wanted his life back, and he'd done what he had to do to get the job done. She could still feel his hands on her, taste him, smell him on her skin. Her stomach rolled. She'd trusted him to help her forget, but all he'd done was make the nightmare worse. "And sleeping with me? Was that part of your sick mind game, too?"

"No. That was never part of the plan. But no matter how many times I tried to tell myself otherwise, I couldn't keep my hands off you, angel." He reached out with one hand as though he intended to comfort her. "You're the strongest, most intelligent—"

"Don't." Her order came out between gritted teeth. He'd lied to her, used her. He wasn't the man she thought he was. He'd seen an easy target and taken advantage, but she was the one filled with shame. Gravity pulled at her, urging her to sink to the floor, but she wouldn't show weakness in front of him. Never again. Another wave of loss swallowed her whole. "I'm not your angel. You don't get to call me sweet nicknames and make this all okay. You don't get to touch me. You don't get to pretend what you did wasn't wrong."

He didn't get to pretend she wasn't grieving all over again.

He dropped his hand, pulled back his shoulders. His expression locked into place, mirroring those times when he hadn't been able to talk about his work for the FBI. She should've recognized that look for what it really was before now—pure apathy. That was what had made him such a good agent, made him the investigator his superiors could rely on, no matter the case. He'd kept himself just distant enough to not let the darkness in, and he was doing the exact same thing to her now—distancing himself. "Who sent you the photos?" he asked.

"Special Agent Dominic. Looks like you weren't the only person in my life lying to my face." Dominic had obviously known Declan was alive before setting eyes on him in her office. He'd been surveilling her husband for a few weeks.

But why? Why was everyone keeping secrets? This was her life, damn it. She deserved the truth. She ripped her cargo jacket from her shoulder, biting down against the pain where the Hunter's arrow had pierced her, and shoved the coat into him on her way toward the bedroom door. "You can have this back. I don't need it anymore."

Footsteps closed in behind her, then a strong hand on her arm spun her into his chest. "Kate—"

"I told you not to touch me." She wrenched out of his grip, put a few feet of space between them. The anger distorted into an all-too-familiar choking sensation. She couldn't breathe. Couldn't think. "Whether you're the husband I buried after the shooting or the man who pulled me from that pit,

I don't care. Don't follow me, don't insert yourself back into my life and don't try to apologize. I don't ever want to see you again."

She had to get out of there, away from him. Not waiting for his response, Kate headed for the front door. Hundreds of Christmas lights and decorations blurred in her peripheral vision, but where she'd had happy, comforting memories to draw from at the sight, now a tainted mass of betrayal set up residence. She grabbed her overnight bag and wrenched the thick front door open, stepping out into the freezing Alaskan night, and slammed the door behind her.

He let her go.

Her heated breath froze on the air, forming crystalized puffs in front of her mouth. Cold worked into her lungs and cleared her head.

Dominic was waiting on her. They were going to have a talk about how he got ahold of those surveillance photos of Declan. But she couldn't let the past few minutes—days—get to her. Despite the situation between her and Declan, she had a job to do, too. Another woman had presumably gone missing. She wouldn't let the new cracks in her armor affect the case. Not again.

The stairs protested under her weight as she forced her way to the SUV. They weren't far up the mountain. Once the sun rose, Declan could make his way back to the city on his own. She wasn't coming back here. She hit the button on her key fob to start the engine, and it roared to life. Climbing inside, she hauled her bag into the passenger seat and cranked the heater.

Snow popped and groaned beneath the vehicle's tires as she headed down the mountain. Every foot gained away from that cabin—away from him—released the pressure building around her heart.

But halfway down, the lights on the console flickered. Same with the headlights as the SUV's RPMs sank to zero. The engine died, and Kate pressed her foot against the brake pedal. Pitch blackness filled the interior of the vehicle as she rolled to a stop. Pressing the start button, she listened for a sign of what might be wrong with the engine. "Come on."

The battery must've died from the dropping temperatures. Lucky for her, Sullivan Bishop required every member of the Blackhawk Security team to carry extra ammunition, weapons, first aid kits, survival gear and an additional car battery. Never knew what kind of mess their clients or the weather would get them into, and it was always better to be prepared than caught unaware.

Pulling her phone from her jacket pocket, she sent a quick message to the team. She was back on the Hunter's case, at least for now, and she'd need their help. She tossed the phone into the passenger seat, then unholstered her weapon, checked the magazine and loaded a fresh round into the chamber. Shoving it back into her shoulder holster, she pushed open the door with her uninjured arm and hit the small dirt road.

With a single glance into the surrounding trees, Kate walked to the back of the SUV and squeezed the lever for the tailgate. No sign Declan had followed her. The last thing she needed was for him to come out here to try to help. The muscles in her jaw ached. He'd done enough damage for one day.

The soft hissing of the tailgate's hydraulics drowned the steady sounds of the great outdoors. Hauling the battery and an extra flashlight from the back, she swung open the driver's-side door and popped the hood, her boots slipping on the thin layer of compacted snow.

How long had he been surveilling her, studying her? Kate blinked to clear the burning from her eyes as she hefted the SUV's hood. Following her?

Streaks of green and purple painted the sky in rivulets overhead, each strand branching off from a central point as the aurora danced in full display tonight. Millions of stars peppered through the thin veil of color, only adding a minuscule amount of light for her to see the vehicle's engine. Clenching the flashlight between her teeth, she twisted the bolts of the dead battery free with a wrench.

She was scheduled to meet Dominic in thirty minutes. Every minute counted when a victim went missing, and the longer she was out here, the less chance the FBI—the less chance Kate—had of finding the Hunter's latest victim alive.

Kate wrapped her fingers around the flashlight and swiped the back of her hand beneath her running nose. Hell, it was cold. Rubbing her hands together, she blew hot air into her palms in an effort to keep circulation moving. She'd close this case, she'd move on with her life, and she'd help those clients she could. Without Declan.

Within a few minutes, the new battery was in place, and she settled in behind the wheel. Kate pushed the start button.

Silence.

"Are you kidding me?" What else could be wrong with the damn thing? She glanced in the rearview mirror, back up the road toward the cabin. She was going to have to go back up there, going to have to confront Declan again while she waited for a tow truck and a ride-share to make it to her meeting with Dominic. The other option was freezing to death.

Kate shook her head. Okay. Maybe freezing to death wasn't such a bad idea right about now.

She sensed movement from the back seat, and she automatically reached for the gun in her holster. A stinging pain pinched at her neck as a gloved hand closed over her mouth.

She wrapped her fingers around her gun's grip, but her body grew heavier with every pump of her heart. She couldn't get it out of the holster. Panic flooded her as the hand slipped from her mouth and took the weapon straight from her holster.

"Can't have you ending the fun before it begins." A black ski mask appeared in her rearview mirror as her eyes grew heavy. Darkness crept around the edges of her vision, then pulled her down into blackness as the drugs took effect.

"You're mine, Kate, and nobody is going to take you from me this time."

SHE WAS DECLAN'S weakness, always had been.

Now she was gone. She'd wanted him at his lowest, and he'd thrown it in her face. By holding her away from the truth in an effort to keep her in his life, he'd only managed to push her away.

Declan held on to the cargo jacket she'd pushed at his chest, his fingers poking through the hole over the left breast. Where their killer had pierced her shoulder with an arrow. He was still out there, still hunting. Declan rolled the side of his mouth between his teeth and bit until blood spread over his tongue. What kind of bastard did he have to be to lie to the only woman who'd been willing to help him, to trust him? He was a damn fool.

And for what? A few more details on a life that didn't matter? He was never going to be the man she'd married. Even if every memory that'd been stripped from his head came rushing back, too much had changed since then. He'd changed.

"Damn it." She shouldn't be out there alone. If he left now, he could catch up, ensure she was safe until she reached her meeting with Dominic. Then he and his former partner could have a talk about boundaries. Sending Kate those surveillance photos had crossed a line. But in the end, he was as guilty as Dominic. He'd watched her apartment, memorized her routines, investigated her clients. He'd learned everything he could about her before stepping foot in the house that night to ensure she hadn't been involved in the shooting. It had all been part of the plan.

Only, he hadn't expected to fall for her in the process.

Declan strode to the cabin's guest bedroom, shoving his arms into his coat along the way. He'd have to make sure to thank Kate's teammate for preparing for the apocalypse next time he saw Vincent. Arming himself with a handgun, a fresh magazine and a burner phone from the stash of supplies, Declan loaded a round into the barrel, checked the safety and holstered the weapon.

Kate could still be a target. Adrenaline surged through him. He'd promised to protect her, and he'd keep that promise until the Hunter was in cuffs or dead.

He'd seen the shadows in her eyes, the fear in her movements since he'd pulled her out of that damn pit. The nightmares haunted him, too. He wasn't going to let that son of a bitch touch her. Not again.

He hit the cabin's front steps and followed the missing SUV's tire tracks leading to the one-lane route down the mountain. Snow crunched beneath his boots as the light show of the aurora borealis lit the way. Cold worked through his thick layers and straight into his bones, tensing his muscles into a constant ache. Or was it the fact he'd only ever felt warm—felt whole—when Kate was near?

Hell, he should've told her the truth before now, but it was too late. There was no going back, and he feared she'd never forgive him.

He picked up the pace. No movement in the trees on either side of the road, but he wasn't going to relax, either. Not until he found Kate.

Dropping temperatures stiffened his fingers. Moonlight filtered through the trees ahead where the road disappeared. If she'd already gotten to the main road, he'd lose her forever. No. He couldn't think about that right now.

A flashlight beam caught his notice down the road. One hundred feet, maybe less. No other movement. No sign of Kate. Declan pulled the gun from his holster and slowed his pace. The hairs on the back of his neck rose. He stopped in the middle of the road, listened. Was that the sound of an engine? Taking cover behind a tree, he stared straight into the darkness on the other side of the road and tabbed off the safety of his sidearm.

Keeping to the trees, he raised his weapon as he headed in the direction he thought the sound was coming from. But the outline of an SUV separated from the shadows, and something inside of him caught fire. He knew that vehicle, and there was absolutely no reason why it would be sitting there. "Kate."

He pumped his legs hard, lungs burning for oxygen. The driver's-side door had been left open, the flashlight discarded on the ground. His fingers trailed over the freezing metal as he slid to a stop beside the driver's seat. No, no, no, no. This was wrong. Kate wouldn't abandon the vehicle in the middle of the night in these temperatures. She wouldn't have walked away. Which meant…

Declan searched the interior of the vehicle, recovering her phone and overnight bag in the passenger seat, and a syringe in the back. His mouth dried, his breath frozen in midair. The son of a bitch had been waiting for her in the back seat. He'd drugged her. Put his hands on her.

Rage exploded behind his sternum. He snapped his attention to the tree line as he let it take control. "He took her."

It had been the sound of an engine before. The unsub was in the middle of making his escape. Pocketing her phone, Declan circled the vehicle, heading straight into the trees.

One set of deep footprints had left distinct marks in the snow but disappeared only a few meters past the tree line. The smell of gasoline mixed with exhaust hung in the air. Impossible to drive a car or SUV through these trees. But an ATV? If the Hunter knew these woods as well as he knew the ones surrounding Michaels's cabin, he could get in and out without anybody knowing.

Declan swept the flashlight beam at his feet and spotted the two lines of a distinct tread pattern. The ATV would've had to have been in position before the suspect got into Kate's vehicle. Question was, how did the bastard get her to stop at this precise location? Had he injected her with whatever was in that syringe while the vehicle was still moving? Seemed risky. She could've veered into any one of these trees, and she'd put the SUV in Park.

He twisted his gaze back to the abandoned vehicle. Smaller footprints circled around the back of the SUV. No. The attacker would have had to get her to stop some other way. The only other option was sabotaging the engine somehow.

Her abduction hadn't been rushed or a moment of panic like before. Whoever had taken her had planned this out.

Declan fanned his grip over the warming metal of the gun and headed deeper into the woods. The man would've wanted her separated from any kind of support or backup.

"I'm going to find you, Kate." Digging her phone from his jacket pocket, he sent her team an SOS message and tossed the device back toward the SUV. Blackhawk Security had the tech to track her phone. They'd do their jobs, and he'd do his. Gritting his teeth, he left the vehicle and her belongings behind.

His eyes adjusted to the shadows. Every instinct flared warning, but he pushed them to the back of his mind. The Hunter had taken his life from him, and he'd do whatever it took to get that back. "I'm not letting you go."

Branches scratched at his face and neck as he followed the treads in the snow. Thick trees barely allowed any moonlight through, but Declan wasn't afraid of the dark. He'd lived there long enough, and he'd keep living there until Kate was back in his arms. Where she belonged.

A few hundred feet past the tree line, his boot hit something solid and metal. The device snapped closed at his feet. A bear trap. Crouching down, he flipped the mass of metal upside down and moonlight glinted off another rig a few feet away. Over two-hundred pounds of force waiting to break one of his legs. The ATV's tire treads had swerved around what look like an entire minefield of bear traps. How long had the bastard been planning this?

A gruff laugh burst from Declan. He stood, shouting into the blackness ahead, "Is that the best you've got!"

Silence.

"That's what I thought." As long as he kept inside the tracks, he'd avoid getting his leg snapped in half. Question was, how many other traps had the Hunter set?

In reality, it didn't matter. He'd stay the course. He'd get Kate back. That was what partners did for each other. They protected one another, had each other's backs. He couldn't go back to the way it was before. In the dark without his memories. Alone. She'd changed all that, and he wasn't ready to let her go.

His Kate. His past. His present. His future.

The aurora above shifted, greens and purples reaching down through the trees, outlining the single man standing in the ATV's treads ahead. Black clothing, black hood over his head and the gleam of a silver blade in his hand.

"Kenneth Winter." The stitches in Declan's side stretched with a deep inhale.

The scent of gasoline strengthened, and he slowed, twisted his wrist to make the gun in his hand more visible. This wasn't going to be a fair fight. Where was the ATV? Where was Kate? She was the unsub's most prized possession. The son of a bitch wouldn't let her out of his sight for long. She had to be close by. Declan stepped forward. "I warned you not to touch her again. Now you're going to pay for what you've done."

"Care to make a bet, Monroe?" The distorted voice echoed off the surrounding trees, and Declan froze. Bet?

Brandishing the knife in filtered moonlight, the bastard cocked his head to one side. "You lost the last round. Would be such a shame if you lost two times in a row. Especially with Kate's life on the line."

"This isn't a game to me." Declan raised the gun and aimed, pulling the trigger.

One second, the suspect had been there. The next, the bullet penetrated a tree right where the Hunter had been standing. Damn it. Where was the son of a bitch?

Declan scanned the trees, taking cover behind a large pine to his right. Freezing air burned going down his throat as he listened for movement. "All right. You want to play? Let's play."

The hunt had only begun.

Chapter Thirteen

The more she swallowed around the gag in her mouth, the drier her throat seemed to get. Kate pulled at her wrists but only managed to tighten the rope around her neck. The last thing she remembered before waking up hog-tied to this chair...

The SUV had died on the way to her meeting with Dominic. Her abductor had been in the back seat the entire time.

She blinked against the brightness of the single bare bulb above her head. He'd drugged her, and she couldn't remember anything after that. Not how he'd gotten her here. Not where they were.

Studying the medium-size cabin, she memorized the layout. She'd been placed with her back to the door at one end of the main room, a table straight ahead holding a crossbow a few feet away. Exposed roof slats, cobwebs, wood-burning stove, old furniture covered in nothing but dust. Shelves lined with food cans showed their age. Nobody had lived here in a long time.

Which meant nobody would have reason to look for her here either.

Heavy footfalls shook the hardwood floor beneath her, then a gust of wind burst through the front door as it swung open. Speckles of dust clouded the air around her. "I was starting to wonder if I'd given you too much sedative."

That voice. His voice. The man who'd taken her.

Nausea churned in her gut as the door slammed shut. As far as she could tell, there was one way in and one way out. She'd have to go through him to get to it.

Kate twisted her head as far to one side as she could, but the rope around her throat only cut off her air supply further. A shiver chased up her spine, raising the hairs on the back of her neck as he moved into her peripheral vision. The fabric gag had gone soggy in her mouth, impossible to move. She forced herself to breathe evenly, to study him. To find his weakness. Because she wasn't going to die in here. She tugged at her wrists again when the gag suppressed her question. Where was Declan?

"Promise not to scream?" The Hunter crouched low on his haunches in front of her, like the predator he was, waiting for the perfect moment to strike.

The evidence suggested Special Agent Kenneth Winter had worked all four of the missing persons cases the Hunter's victims were tied to. He'd taken those women, seduced them and set them free in the wilderness before he started his hunt. The man had been in her office, gotten to know her when she and Dominic had met to discuss cases. Had it all been a means to an end? A way to get close to her?

He reached toward her, and she jerked away. "Up to you, Kate."

A groan escaped up her throat as the rope burned across the delicate skin over her neck and wrists. She wouldn't scream, but she'd do far, far worse when she got free of these ropes. The psychopath in front of her had killed four innocent women that she knew of as well as Michaels. Her former patient had been a pawn in his sick game. She wasn't going to let him get away with it.

She had to focus, had to plan. The predator in front of her matched Agent Winter's build, same low tone when he spoke, same dark eyes. This was the man who'd thrown her in that pit and hung Declan from his feet to die.

The Hunter had stayed one step ahead of her and the FBI this entire investigation, but there was a reason Sullivan had handpicked her to profile killers for his team. Kate had the ability to know exactly what they wanted. Nine times out of ten it was simply control—over their victims, over their emotions, over their own traumatic pasts. But this one... He wanted to prove himself. Prove he could beat her.

With her attention on that damn ski mask and the slight bulge of the voice distorter over his neck, she wrapped her fingers into fists. And nodded.

"That's my girl." He raised his hand again, the brush of his coarse knuckles against her cheek nauseating. The tang of cologne worked deep into her system, and her nostrils burned. Too sharp. Nothing like Declan's subtle, masculine scent. Her bottom lip rolled with the gag as he slid the soaked rag beneath her chin.

She needed him closer. Mouthing her question, she closed her eyes as though she were still affected by the drugs, and he leaned in slightly. Another inch, and she'd get her shot at knocking him out cold. The overhead light reflected off the blade holstered to his hip, but until she had her hands freed, it wouldn't do her a damn bit of good. There had to be something else she could use to cut through the rope.

"You know, I've studied you, Kate. I've gotten to know you over these past few months. I know your routines, the way you profile your targets, watched you grieve after losing your husband." The Hunter closed the small space between them as heat built in her chest. "Do you really think headbutting me is going to give you an advantage?"

"I wasn't going to headbutt you." Shoving down through her toes, she pushed herself and the chair off the hardwood floor and launched herself straight into him. They landed in a heap on the floor, but the wooden chair she'd been tied to didn't even splinter. She hit the floor hard, landing on her side. Panic flared as he stood and took position above her, one foot pressed against her shin bone tied to the chair.

Pain screamed up her leg and down into her toes, but she had to find something—anything—to cut through the ropes while she had the chance. Her fingers splayed out, grasping into thin air, desperate for contact. All she needed—

"A few more pounds of pressure is all it would take to break your leg, Kate, but I don't want to hurt you more than I have to. So, please, don't give me a reason." A deep, evil laugh penetrated the ski mask as he wrenched her upright. Fisting one length of rope, he leveled his face with hers and pulled until the coarse strands cut into her. "You know why I killed them, don't you? All those women."

"Me…" She struggled to breathe. She couldn't push the air out her mouth fast enough. Her dull rasping reached her ears. A wave of dizziness washed through her head, and all she could think about in that moment was her own survival.

And Declan. He'd lied to her, made her believe he was someone he wasn't, but every cell in her body screamed for him right now. She'd trusted him. Hell, she'd fallen for him, and she didn't want their conversation to be the last thing she ever said to him. Because when it came right down to it, he'd been the one to pull her from the soul-sucking agony of grief, to make her feel again, to care. He'd taken a bullet for her, rescued her from the bottom of that pit when she believed nobody would find her. Loved her when she was at her darkest. And she loved him, too. "To beat…me."

"No, Kate." Another laugh pooled dread at the base of her spine. He loosened his grip on the rope, and she was able to take her first full breath since slamming him to the floor. Grabbing the ski mask at the crown of his head, the Hunter pulled the fabric from his face. He peeled the voice distorter from his throat. "I killed them to show you I'm the one who can protect you from the monsters out there in the world. Not Declan. Not Blackhawk Security or your team. Me."

No longer framed by the ski mask, familiar brown eyes stared back at her. Confusion tore through her. No. It wasn't possible. The sedative had to still be in her system. It was messing with her head, making her hallucinate. There was no way he'd been behind all those attacks. "Ryan."

"Surprise." The small mole on the left side of his chin shifted with a smile, but where she'd been comforted by that smile in the past, only fear built in her gut now. "Gotta tell you, Kate, feels good finally letting you in on the truth. Now we can start fresh."

"You sent Michaels to the house." She licked her dry lips. The pieces were slowly falling into place as the sedatives burned off. She had to keep him talking. Long enough for her to form a new plan. "You made him obsessed with me to the point he'd kill Declan. Then you sent him again when you discovered Declan was alive all this time." She didn't understand. "You were my friend. You helped me through my grief, you were—"

"I was there for you, Kate. For over a year while you grieved. Then I discovered my former partner—a man who was supposed to be dead, by the way—had been walking around the city without a damn clue who he was, but I knew. I knew he'd make his way back to you and destroy all of the progress I'd made."

His voice rose. "I was the one who checked in on you every night after work. I was the one who brought you takeout when you couldn't bring yourself to get out of bed. I was the one who convinced you to go back to work, to take off that damn wedding ring, to put yourself first for once. Me. Not him."

Dominic straightened, turning toward the old woodstove, the butt of his knife within reaching distance. He took a deep breath. If she could only get her hands free…

"You know, I was so nervous when I saw Declan in your office a few days ago, I almost drew my weapon and finished the job right then and there." Glancing back at her, the special agent tossed the mask and distorter into the burning stove. "See, he suspected me back before that first shooting. I could tell. It was this look he gave me during one of our other serial cases, the kind that said he'd figured out what I like to do in my spare time, and I couldn't afford him interrupting my plans for you. Turns out, I didn't need to worry. Declan can't remember anything, and that leaves us all the time in world."

For what?

"You found the women through missing persons cases you and your partner worked," Kate said. "You got close to them, seduced them. Then you set them free in the woods and hunted them down like animals." The last word sneered from her mouth. Kate tugged at her wrists, careful not to pull too hard to engage the rope around her neck. Was that the rope loosening? Her teeth clenched against the groan working up her throat as the burns around her wrists protested with each movement. "You're a coward. That's why you brought in Michaels to do your dirty work, isn't it? You were too afraid to confront Declan on your own."

"You're trying to make me angry. Maybe hoping I'll lash out and knock you over so you can search for something to cut through your ropes," he said. "It's very clever, but you've already forgotten, I know your strategies, Kate. I know you. And I've waited too long for this to spoil all the fun in one night."

"What about Special Agent Winter?" Kate felt the rope give, and she struggled to worm one hand free. Progress. "You set him up to take the fall, didn't you? Just another pawn in your game."

"It's true Kenneth worked all of those cases, but what the official reports don't say is that we worked them as a team. I suggested he take the lead to get his shot at a nice promotion while I scouted for my next target. Win-win. You have no idea how many cases I had to dredge through to find witnesses who looked like you, because let's be honest, you're one of a kind."

Dominic hefted the large crossbow from a table to her right and loaded a bolt. He ran his fingers down the shaft. "Whether you realize it or not, Kate, our fates are intertwined. Ever since I first met you, I knew I had to have you for myself. I've got plans for you."

He lowered the barrel of the crossbow into his other hand and aimed at the floor as he closed the distance between them. "I'm not about to spoil any more surprises."

Care to make a bet, Monroe?

What the hell had the bastard been talking about? A bet?

Sweat dripped down Declan's spine as he wound through the trees. The ATV's tracks left lighter impressions here, the ground harder with the frost, but he wouldn't give up. He wouldn't slow down. Not until Kate was safe. Exhaustion pulled at him, his breath heavier than a few minutes ago. Those words echoed through his head over and over.

The tracks disappeared in the thick of fallen foliage.

Damn it. Scanning the surrounding area, he searched for a spot they might pick up. Twenty feet out. Thirty. The ground had frozen solid. He was searching for a needle in a haystack now, in the dark. The howls of a nearby wolf pack shot his instincts into overdrive, and he tightened his grip on the gun. Sliding his hand over his wound, he exhaled hard at the feel of wet gauze and fabric. "Yeah. That looks about right."

Blood.

The wolves had probably smelled him a mile

away, mistaking him for an injured animal. They weren't wrong. Hell, he barely had the energy to keep himself standing as dropping temperatures stole his body heat. The chances of a wolf attack were slim, but the addition of his wound didn't help. He had a higher chance of freezing to death at this rate, but he'd keep moving.

Serial killers are like wolves, Monroe. They'll go to elaborate lengths to get what they want, but they'll never die for their cause.

Declan slowed as recognition flared at the voice in his head. Special Agent Ryan Dominic. Right. They'd been partners before he'd lost his memory.

Crystalized puffs of air formed in front of his mouth, and he curled the fingers of his free hand to hold on to as much heat as he could. A quick flash of memory streaked like lightning across his mind.

Him and Dominic looking at a whiteboard covered in photos and evidence. A murder board. Five victim photos had been taped to the surface, lines connecting the dots between the pictured women. They'd been hunting another serial killer then. What was the moniker they'd given him?

Declan rubbed at his eyes as a dull pain filled his skull.

The Alaskan Logger. Their unsub had taken to copycatting the Anchorage Lumberjack, who was later revealed to have been killed by his son, Sullivan Bishop, aka Sebastian Warren, the founder and CEO of Blackhawk Security, of all people.

The Alaskan Logger had taken five women

who'd rejected his advances, killing them with the ax he'd worked the land with, as the Lumberjack had. Declan and Dominic were closing in on the Logger's identity when the unsub went cold.

Care to make a bet, Monroe? I'll give you five to one odds the Logger isn't finished, Dominic had said. *Come on, we'll make a game of it.*

Declan snapped his head up, not really seeing the trees around him. Son of a bitch. Dominic. Reaching for the burner he'd stashed in his pocket, he dialed Blackhawk's main number. The line rang once. And again.

His heart threatened to pound straight out of his chest as more memories rushed forward from the darkness locked inside his head. Pinching the bridge of his nose, he shut his eyes tight against the pain, but the fragments kept coming. A growl ripped up his throat.

He and Dominic on the office's annual hunting trip. His partner's favored crossbow. The file Declan had started building when the first two women had been discovered shot through the heart with an arrow. Declan had connected the dots mere hours before Michaels had shot up his house. He'd found evidence. He just couldn't remember what it had been.

Another memory slipped into his mind, cutting through the violence, and the breath left his lungs. A positive pregnancy test. Kate's smile as she bounded into his arms with the news. She'd wrapped her legs around his waist and crushed her mouth to his right there in the middle of their living room.

Declan blinked against the burn in his eyes. Warmth spread through him, combating the freezing cold around him. He wiped the back of his hand beneath his nose. He would've been a father if Kate hadn't been shot.

Every minute wasted was another minute the chances of Kate returning home alive dropped, and he couldn't handle the thought of finding her out here, alone, with an arrow through her chest.

A soft click registered over the phone, and he said, "Put me through to Elizabeth Dawson. Now."

He should've seen it sooner. Taking Kate off the case, sending her the surveillance photos, setting the meeting. It was all part of Dominic's plan to get her alone. Isolated. To take her from Declan. Hell, he should've trusted his instincts the first time the bastard walked into Kate's office.

"Dawson," a familiar voice said.

A small wave of relief flooded him. "Elizabeth, it's Declan."

"Where are you? Kate's vehicle is here down the road from Vincent's cabin, but we can't find her anywhere." Fear laced the network expert's voice. "There's a syringe, her phone is here on the side of the road, we've got two sets of footprints and the engine's been tampered with. What is going on?"

"The Hunter is Dominic. He took her. I can't go into how I know. I need you to trust me. I'm going to get her back." His lungs spasmed from the cold.

He had to believe that. The alternative… Declan shook his head. No. There was no alternative. He loved her, damn it. He needed her, and there was no way in hell he'd give up on them. They'd been through too much together, and he wasn't ready to let her go. Wasn't ready to let the history between them go. "I need you to work your magic and tell me where he is."

"The FBI agent working the Hunter case is the killer? Give me a second." Static crackled across the line, then a hard thump as though Elizabeth had set the phone down. "You're on speaker. I've got Anthony and Elliot with me, too."

"Good. He has no reason to suspect we know his real identity so there's a chance he has his Bureau-issued phone on him. Also, tell me if Dominic or anyone he might've investigated has property out here," Declan said. "He took off through the woods on an ATV, but I've lost the tracks. Those things only hold a few hours of gas at a time. He couldn't have gone far."

The chances Declan would get handed a property with the killer's name on it were slim, but the phone was a promising lead. Dominic was smart, organized. He'd stayed ahead of Blackhawk Security and the FBI this entire time without raising any warnings, but his former partner had never gotten on Declan's bad side before. Chaos was about to reign.

Declan turned around, scanning the shadows. Another drop of sweat slid down his neck. He had to control his body temperature. The slightest hint of moisture could pull his system into hypothermic territory.

The line crackled again. Then silence. "Have Elliot collect as much evidence as he can from the vehicle," Declan said. "We need to have a case built when this goes sideways." Because it most definitely would. Dominic was FBI—he knew the system—and Declan wouldn't be surprised if the bastard had a backup plan to get himself out of a conviction. One that looked a hell of a lot like Special Agent Kenneth Winter taking the fall.

No answer. "Elizabeth?"

Pulling the phone from his ear, he watched as a bar dropped off the screen. He was out in the middle of the damn wilderness. Barely any coverage. He was lucky his call had gone through at all but pinning Dominic's location depended on staying in range. His fingers squeezed around the phone. "Elizabeth!"

"Got—phone." Static filled his ears.

Seconds passed. A combination of frustration and panic spread through him as bits and pieces of Elizabeth's voice punctured the white noise.

"—have his position. Declan?—me? He's— quarter mile north of you. We're on our—"

"Quarter mile north." Declan pocketed the phone and ran as fast as he could. His muscles burned with exertion, but he pushed through. Nothing would keep him from getting to Kate. Not the freezing cold. Not hypothermia. Not a pack of hunting wolves. And certainly not some son of a bitch who'd taken the only person who mattered to Declan in this life.

She'd brought him out of the darkness of his past, given him everything he could've imagined and more. Gifted him with her strength, with her body, with hope. He wasn't going to turn his back on that or on her.

Fallen trees and razor-sharp pieces of ice threatened to trip him up, but Declan only pushed himself harder when a single cabin came into view up ahead.

Partially obstructed by massive tress on every side, the small wood structure wouldn't have been visible in spring or summer, but because of the lack of leaves, the roof peeked through the trees. A perfect hideout for a serial killer. Off the beaten path, no longer in the residential or rental rotation as far as he could tell from the state of the place.

Fogged windows decreased visibility inside as Declan took position within the ring of trees surrounding the cabin, but a dim light inside revealed there was condensation bubbling at the bottom of each pane of glass. Someone was home. Moss and vines climbed the dilapidated wood stairs, slats pulling away from the overall frame. A single step onto that tilted porch would give away his presence. He had to find another way in.

Keeping low, Declan crouched as he moved from tree to tree for a better angle, gun tight in his grip.

One shot. That was all it would take to end this nightmare.

He switched off his flashlight, relying solely on the single burning bulb glowing through the south window. No movement from inside, but that didn't mean anything. Didn't mean Dominic had already finished with Kate and moved on to his next victim. Didn't mean he wasn't here at all. Or that the cabin was a trap.

Declan sat back on his haunches and extracted the phone from his jacket. No coverage. No calling in for backup. He was on his own.

Her muted scream drove him into action.

Declan raced across the dirt and bounded up the stairs. No time to test the lock. Hiking his foot beside the rustic doorknob, he put everything he had into a solid kick. The door swung open, hinges protesting as he filled the doorway. Pain ricocheted up his thigh and into his bullet wound, but faded with one look at Kate bound in the chair, her back to him.

"Kate." He raised the gun and silently shifted across the floor. No sign of Dominic. The bastard had to be around here somewhere. "I'm here, angel, and I'm taking you home."

Chapter Fourteen

"Declan, no!" The gag had been put back in place, rendering her warning useless. He didn't understand. The entire abduction, having her here, it was all part of the plan. Part of the trap Dominic had set for him.

Kate pulled at the remaining rope around her wrists as Declan moved deeper into the cabin. She bounced in the chair, trying to knock it over, to get his attention, to do anything to make him get out of here. She could barely see him out of the corner of her eye as she twisted her head, her back to the door. Her throat burned as she screamed as loud as she could. "Stop!"

A solid kick from Dominic standing behind one of the canning shelves sent Declan's gun flying across the floor, the thump of metal against wood loud in her ears.

Drawing a noose around Declan's neck, Dominic pulled him tight against him. Canned goods hit the hardwood floor as both men struggled for the upper hand. A hit to Declan's face brought him down onto one knee, then another. Another after that. Dominic wouldn't let up.

Panic flared in Kate's chest as Declan took hit after hit with no sign of getting to his feet. Then, swinging his leg out wide, Declan unbalanced Dominic and pushed him backward, the noose still tied around his neck.

Kate kicked at the chair, a rough growl escaping from around the wet fabric in her mouth. She kicked again, but the rope only grew tighter around her neck. She had to get out of this chair. She had to help him. She scanned the dusty table for a weapon or something she could use to cut the rope, but Dominic had taken the crossbow to wait for Declan. Blood-chilling silence filled the cabin, and she wrenched around for a better look.

Dominic held on to the noose, one hand at the base of Declan's neck pressed into the wall, the other pulling the rope taut. The sound of glass shattering filled the cabin, heavy breaths barely noticeable over the hard pound of her heartbeat behind her ears.

Declan threw one punch, which Dominic dodged, and hauled his elbow back for another. Dominic landed a solid hit, and Declan fell backward against the canning shelves, giving the Hunter another chance to tighten the rope around her husband's neck.

"Leave him alone!" Another garbled shout. She couldn't see them well. Swinging her head from side to side, she struggled to get Declan back in her sights, but the binds around her body made it impossible. Clawing at the rope around her wrists, Kate ignored the stinging pain of burned skin.

A hard thump broke through the air, then another. Nausea churned in her gut. She forced herself to breathe, to think.

Movement pulled her attention to one side as Dominic dragged a bloodied and swaying Declan into her peripheral vision. No. She wasn't going to lose him again. Not like this. Not ever. Rough exhales flared her nostrils. "Declan, get up!" she tried to yell. "Get up!"

"You couldn't beat me before you lost your memories, Monroe, and you can't beat me now." Dominic stared straight at her, waited for her full attention as he slammed her husband into the floor. Dominic dragged Declan back toward the door, throwing the noose over one of the exposed beams running through the cabin.

Rage exploded through her, and she snapped her head to face front. Dominic had taken everything. Her psychology practice, her confidence, her house, her baby. He wouldn't take Declan from her, too. Clenching her fists, Kate pressed her toes into the floor and rocked back on the chair's hind legs. She used the momentum to rocket her forward, just as she'd done when she tackled Dominic to the floor. Forcing one bound foot in front of the other toward the table on the other side of the room, she turned ninety degrees.

No, no, no, no.

Inhaling deep, Kate shoved off with everything she had, sending the back of the chair straight into the edge of the table. A scream worked up her throat as pain splintered down her spine and across her shoulders. The chair shattered around her, loosening the ropes. She pulled the gag from around her mouth and dove to wrap her hand around one of the chair legs as the ropes fell to the floor.

Strong arms wrapped around her, constricting her movements. "I'm not finished with you, Kate."

Slamming her head back into Dominic's face, she took advantage as he dropped his hold, and swung the chair leg as hard as she could. Wood met bone in a sickening crunch.

She lunged for Declan, but then the Hunter nearly tackled her to the floor. Her muscles burned as she battled to stay upright. Gripping his two middle fingers, she wrenched them back as hard as she could with one hand and swallowed a pain-filled scream as she swung the chair leg into his side. The arrow wound in her shoulder cried for relief, but Dominic was using his weight against her.

She hit the floor hard and kicked upward, landing a hit to his chest. "Ryan, please. You don't have to do this. We can get you help. I can help."

But it wasn't enough. The Hunter stumbled backward. A growl ripped up his throat as he reached for her, but a rope sliding around his neck cut him off.

Declan hauled his former partner into him, blood dripping down his face. "You don't get to touch her."

Relief surged through her at seeing Declan alive, but it was short-lived.

Lifting his legs high, Dominic threw his weight forward as she'd done with the chair. The bare bulb above highlighted the sweat across Dominic's brow as he flipped Declan over his shoulder and flat on his back on the floor.

The rope fell into a pile at Dominic's feet. Faster than she thought possible, he wrapped his hand around her throat and hefted her into him. "What I need, Kate, is for you to start running. That's my favorite part, you know. The panic in their sobs as they scream for help. The fear in their eyes, but sooner or later, they realize there's nowhere they can hide. Not from me."

"You…broke…them." She couldn't breathe, but one thing was clear as the lack of oxygen took hold: she'd already lost everything that mattered and survived.

Her gaze flickered to the wall of muscle rising behind Dominic. Kate slammed her arm into his forearm, struggling to get free as a distraction, but her injury took the strength out of each hit. Wrenching her elbow back, she went for his face, but he only blocked the hit. She turned as much as she could and thrust her leg backward to escape his grip. In vain. "You can't break me."

"Let's test that theory, shall we?" Violence swam through Dominic's dark eyes a split second before a glass bottle broke against the side of his head. His fingers loosened from around her throat, and Kate stumbled back against the shelf near the door as Declan charged the special agent full force.

Her fingers hit metal on the shelf. The crossbow. Adrenaline fueled her enough to heft the weapon from the shelf, and she took aim. Her hands and wrists burned as feeling came back, but she slipped her finger over the trigger.

Both men battled for the upper hand, each covered in blood. She didn't have a shot. Declan was too close. Locking her jaw against the pain in her shoulder, she blinked to clear the sweat dripping into her eyes. One wrong move and she'd pierce him instead of Dominic. "Declan, move!"

Her partner ripped away from his opponent and ducked.

Kate pulled the trigger.

A soft whistling filled the cabin, and then Dominic's scream filled her ears as the arrow tore through the muscles in his shoulder. Right where he'd shot her. He folded in half.

Pulling back his elbow, Declan slammed one final hit into the Hunter's face.

Dominic crumpled to the floor, the thick layer of dust disturbed from a hard exhale escaping his lungs as he sank into unconsciousness.

The crossbow grew heavy in her hands, and she let it sink to her side as exhaustion took control. Her lungs heaved, trying to keep up with her racing heartbeat.

The nightmare was over. They'd apprehended the Hunter, and he would serve out the rest of his life behind bars for what he'd done to all those women, to Brian Michaels.

"Kate…" Declan stumbled forward, his voice weak. Blood dripped from his nose and mouth as he reached out for her. He collapsed against her, arms wrapping around her neck, but she kept him upright through pure force of will. "Did he hurt you?"

"No." Gripping the crossbow, she rested her chin against his shoulder and closed her eyes. He was alive. They'd survived. Together. She blinked back the tears as fear, resentment, rage, every emotion she'd held on to over the last year broke free. He'd saved her life—again—but the hurt was still there. The lie he'd forced her to believe was still there. "You came for me. Even after I told you not to."

"I promised to protect you. I might not remember much, but I do remember that." His words rumbled through his chest and vibrated down to her bones. The ache in her body eased as he pressed his hands against her spine, fitting her against him.

"Thank you." Kate pulled away. He'd saved her life, but everything else? The security she'd felt with him, the connection? The trust? It had all been destroyed. She swiped at her face with her free hand and stepped away. "How did you know where to find me?"

His shoulders sank away from his ears, exhaustion and disappointment clearly etched into his expression. He rolled his lips between his teeth and cast his eyes to the floor. "I remembered something Dominic said to me during an investigation we headed as partners. Then a whole lot more stuff I can't really explain in a way that would make sense. I called your team."

He locked brilliant blue eyes on her. "And I remembered the day you told me about the baby. How happy I was. You told me I was going to be a dad, and I remember thinking life couldn't get any better than that moment. But I was wrong. These last five days, having a second chance..." He stepped closer to her. "You're everything to me, and I don't want to lose you."

Kate shook her head. He already had.

"The worst feeling in the world is knowing you were used and lied to by the person you trusted most in the world," she said. "That's not just going to be fixed with an apology, Declan, and I think the best thing—for both of us—is space. You need to figure out who you are again, what you want to do with your life now that you have that second chance. I need to do the same. I need to learn how to be on my own. Alone. Without grief hanging over my head."

His expression shut down, and she tried to swallow through the hollowness building inside.

Kate swiped at her face again, catching a stray tear on her cheek and backed toward the door. Dominic wasn't dead. He wouldn't stay down for long. "We should call the FBI and Anchorage PD. I need to let my team know what happened."

Declan lifted his hand as though he intended to reach out for her but kept himself in check. "Kate—"

A murderous bellow pierced through the haze clouding her head as Dominic shoved off the floor and lunged.

Her heart caught in her throat, but Declan closed the distance between them, wrapped his fingers around hers and the crossbow and helped her lift the weapon up.

She pulled the trigger.

THE HUNTER WOULD never take another victim again. Would never come after Kate. Special Agent Ryan Dominic was dead.

What was Declan supposed to do now?

He and Kate had had an agreement from the beginning. They would work the case together, then move on with their lives. But this couldn't be it. Not after everything they'd been through. Not after what they'd shared.

Red-and-blue patrol lights highlighted the bruises and scrapes across her angelic face as Declan stalked toward the ambulance where the EMTs checked her wounds. She had to understand. He knew exactly what he wanted. Her.

FBI and Anchorage PD had taken control of the scene. Blackhawk Security was on standby, each member of Kate's team giving their statements. The victims' bodies would be released to their families for burial now that the case of the Hunter was closed. Declan's job was done, but he couldn't leave. Not without her.

"Declan Monroe." A wall of muscle dressed

in a suit stepped into his path, hand outstretched. One of the FBI agents sent to clean up the mess. Cornflower blue eyes scanned him. A five-o'clock shadow and tousled brown hair were evidence of the amount of sleep lost on this case, but somehow Declan knew this agent had never let something as simple as sleep affect his job, which meant they'd known each other. "Special Agent in Charge Mitchell Haynes. You probably don't remember me—"

"You were my boss." Before Declan's entire world had been ripped apart. He remembered that, remembered taking his suspicions about his partner to Haynes only to be told to find hard evidence before making accusations against one of their own. Declan shook the man's hand.

"That's right. Glad to know some of those memories of yours are coming back." Haynes slipped his hands deep in his pants pockets. Mitchell Haynes, the man who'd partnered him with Dominic in the first place. The guy ran an entire team of agents who hunted violent serial offenders on the FBI's most wanted list, but didn't seem to have aged a day over the last year. "I read yours and Ms. Monroe's statements. Everyone else's, too. You successfully tracked and brought down a killer who made it his mission to not leave evidence behind."

"I remember a lot. Have to wonder if you hadn't listened to me before now, none of this would've happened. None of those families would have to bury the women they loved over the next few days." Declan scanned the scene until his gaze landed on

Kate, then nodded toward her. "And she gets the credit here. Couldn't have done any of it without Kate."

Declan maneuvered around Haynes, holding tight to the path to his future. To Kate. Of all the options out there, he didn't want a life that didn't include her. His guardian angel. Over the course of the last five days, she'd become his armor, a part of him, and nothing was worth the cost of losing her.

"Yeah, well. We all make mistakes, right?" Haynes's voice came from behind. "Besides, I knew you'd get your guy, Monroe. You always have. You were my best agent before you got shot. It'd be a shame to see that talent go to waste."

Declan slowed, turned his attention back to the SAC. "What's that supposed to mean?"

"Bringing down the predators is what my team does best, and it's what you're good at." Haynes spread his hands wide, as if that answer was obvious. His voice dropped into graveled territory. "Come back to the FBI, Declan. Help me save hundreds more families the pain of having to lose their loved ones to the sick, violent people set on destroying lives. Help me prevent more women like these four from being abducted, brutalized and murdered."

"You want me to work for the FBI after I killed one of your own men who turned out to be a serial killer?" The weight of Kate's attention squeezed the air in his lungs. This was what he'd worked so hard for over the past year. Finding his place, getting his life back. Remembering who he'd been. Hunting the most violent criminals had been part of him for so long, the idea of settling back into that role bled excitement down his spine.

"You were the only one who suspected Ryan Dominic for what he really was back then. You know the monsters are real, and you're not afraid to face them, Monroe. Only this way, you get to do your job legally." Haynes handed him a card, flashed his straight, white teeth and backed away toward a waiting SUV. "I'll try not to partner you with a serial killer this time. See you in Washington, DC, within the week."

Declan stared at Haynes's name on the small piece of embossed cardstock but couldn't absorb the letters on the card.

"Looks like you got everything you've worked for." Kate still sat at the ambulance, arms folded across her chest. The rope burns had been treated and dressed, but the fact they'd needed treatment at all resurrected the rage for the son of a bitch currently being wheeled out on a stretcher in a body bag from the cabin. "Your memories, your old job. This is great. I'm happy for you."

Not everything. Not yet. Curling his fingers around the card, Declan ignored the chill of the dropping temperatures as her light vanilla scent filled his system. Just one inhale and the fiery burn of revenge ebbed. Would she always have that effect on him or had exhaustion finally caught up? They'd been running off fumes for so long, his body had got-

ten used to the high doses of adrenaline. But now…
Now he wanted nothing more than to take her back
to her apartment and sink into bed for the next several weeks. Taking her hand with his, he ran the pad
of his thumb over her bandages. "Do they hurt?"

"Not as bad as it looks." She wouldn't have ad-
mitted to the pain either way. Always determined
to stand strong, always in control. But Declan knew
the truth. Despite her hardened exterior and attempt
to bury her emotions, in reality, Kate felt entirely
too much. "How's your side?" she asked.

"Medium rare." In truth, he didn't know how the
wound had fared during his fight with Dominic.
He'd refused treatment until Kate had been checked
over first, and his stitches ached with awareness.
The bastard had tried to execute him, but more important, Declan had almost lost her. Again. He'd
failed to protect her from the Hunter, and he'd have
to live with that knowledge for the rest of his life,
but knowing he was the reason she might walk away
now… He couldn't handle that.

"Kate, I'm sorry I lied to you. I didn't want this
to end. I didn't want to lose you. I didn't want…" he
had to be honest with himself "…to be alone again."

The rawness of that admission broke through
in his voice.

She nodded, gaze focused on a point over his
shoulder. "You know, my team has been through a
lot over the last year. Elliot's been shot twice, Sullivan almost died from his injuries and had to be
airlifted to the hospital, Anthony's son was kid-

napped and Elizabeth was abducted when she was four months pregnant with Karina."

She rolled her lips between her teeth as patrol lights reflected off the thin line of water in her eyes. "But no matter what's been thrown at us, we've survived, and we come out on top the next day. Because we trust each other, we rely on one another. Even at this very moment, my team is standing over there waiting to help me with whatever I need from them. There aren't any secrets between us. We all know and have experience with secrets putting lives at risk. I can trust them."

His gut clenched as she turned those green eyes on him, and everything inside of him went cold. This wasn't the woman he'd built the snow fort for, the one he'd taken to bed, the one who'd given him a reason to keep going. No. That woman had a warmth to her gaze. The woman standing in front of him had closed herself off and retreated to the point he wasn't sure he'd ever see that warmth again.

"So we go back to the way it was before? We—" He curled his fingers into his palms, forced himself to breathe through the next words. "We move on."

"That was the plan, wasn't it?" she said. "We'd finish the investigation and continue on like nothing had ever happened." She lifted her chin. "You saved my life—more times than I can count now—and I'll always be thankful for that, but we were partners, Declan. Partners are supposed to trust each other. There shouldn't have been any secrets between us, and I don't think you can promise me there won't be more in the future."

Declan opened his mouth to answer, but no. He couldn't promise her that.

She wiped her hand beneath her nose as she sniffled.

"I thought Ryan Dominic was my friend. Turned out he was a serial killer. I hope you understand that I can't handle any more secrets." Her uninjured shoulder rose on a shrug, the corner of her mouth lifting on one side. Uncrossing her arms, she stepped close to him and placed one hand on his chest, right over his heart.

She lowered that beautiful gaze to his hand and extracted the business card Haynes had left with him. Studying it for a brief moment, she slid it into his pants pocket. "Go get your life back, Declan. You deserve to be happy."

Her fingers feathered over his arm as she stepped around him, her soft vanilla scent still on the air, in his system, becoming part of him. But she'd always been part of him, hadn't she? That wouldn't change. No matter how much distance she put between them.

"Kate." He spun around, his breath icy on the air. "We'll always be unfinished business. Remember that."

Another half smile thinned her lips. "Not this time, Special Agent Monroe."

And then she was gone.

Chapter Fifteen

Six weeks later

She rubbed at the dry skin around her wrists. The Hunter had left his mark. On her body, in her nightmares. Kate stuffed another handful of debris into a large black garbage bag. How many did that make? Sixteen? Seventeen bags?

With the connection between Brian Michaels and Special Agent Ryan Dominic established, the FBI had taken everything they needed to wrap up their investigation, but she still hadn't been able to salvage anything from the house she once considered home. Not even the couch's decorative pillows had survived.

She shoved a featherless pillow into the bag with a little more force than needed, swallowing back the sudden dryness in her throat. It was going to take a lot more than a few garbage bags to get this place ready to sell. She took a deep breath.

Broken glass crunched under her boots as she straightened. A small sting of pain lanced through her shoulder, but the hole from the Hunter's arrow was almost completely healed. Swiping the back of her hand across her forehead, she inhaled deep to clear a rush of dizziness. Exhaustion pulled at her, and bile worked up her throat. Nightmares and heartburn. Great.

She stared out over the remnants of the living room. Not a single piece of furniture, item of clothing or dinner plate had survived both shootings. Insurance would cover the majority of the damage, but this was the second time she'd have to explain why her house had become a crime scene. What a mess—

"Kate," a familiar voice said.

The hairs on the back of her neck rose. Heat flooded her, and she exhaled hard to keep the burn under control. The hits kept on coming. She stuffed another handful of garbage into the sack but didn't turn around. No point. He wasn't staying long. "I figured you'd be across the country by now, assigned to another case."

"I turned down the FBI job." His deep, reserved voice resonated through her, sending a bolt of electricity up her spine. The shifting of broken glass and debris sounded loud in her ears—too loud—as he closed in on her.

"Oh?" The weight of his attention burned between her shoulder blades, but she couldn't face him. The moment she gave in to the urge to lock her gaze on his, the heartache she'd buried over the last month and a half would take control. No.

She was just starting to heal. She couldn't do this again—wouldn't.

Crossing to the other side of the room, Kate scooped the remaining items off her desk into the bag. Broken perfume bottles from his travels all over the world, fractured picture frames holding evidence of the life they once shared. She didn't want any of it. Not anymore. "I thought getting your life back was what you wanted. Going back to the FBI was supposed to help with that."

"It was." Whispers of his exhale tickled over her heated skin. She hadn't heard him move so close. Her body flooded with awareness as his clean, masculine scent worked deep into her lungs. "Until I realized taking that job would mean keeping more secrets from you. And that's the last thing I want."

Air caught in her throat. He'd turned down the job for her? She sagged against the desk, her fingers gripping the edge for support.

"Kate." Declan's fingers fanned over her arm—too familiar, too comforting—and she wanted nothing but to sway into his warmth, trust him, rely on him as she got rid of the evidence of their marriage. But she couldn't. "Look at me."

Her heartbeat thundered behind her ears. Hard to breathe with him so close. His scent filled the space he'd cornered her in, and she couldn't get it out of her system. In all honesty, she hadn't been able to get him out of her system. Not since she'd walked away from him back at the crime scene. It had taken every ounce of energy to keep her distance, to force herself to focus on the next case for Blackhawk, not to wonder if he was safe. If he was alive.

"You're my life, angel. Not getting the rest of my memories back, not some job for the federal government or hunting monsters." His hands circled her waist, pulling her against him. His back pressed against her spine, the even beat of his heart pulsing into her.

She should fight back, but she was just...tired. And he felt so good. His mouth skimmed the shell of her ear. "I stayed away as long as I could to give you the space you wanted, but I choose you. I'm committed to you. No more secrets. No more lies."

Liquid warmth pooled in her stomach and melted her from the inside. That was all she'd ever wanted. Honesty. Safety. Love.

Kate spun in his arms, locked her gaze on those piercing blue eyes. She loved him. More than she'd ever loved another human being. Not the husband she'd buried, not the man who'd saved her life during the investigation but the combination of both. Each had their own strengths, their own weaknesses, but together they formed the man she'd dreamed of spending the rest of her life with. Raising a family with. "What do you want me to say to that?"

"Say yes, Kate." His short burst of laughter ruffled her ponytail. "Say you'll give us a chance to get it right this time."

She stepped out of his reach. Kate bit back the shock of seeing him for the first time in weeks.

Dark circles had taken up residence under his eyes, but his blue gaze remained bright and focused on her. "No more secrets."

"No more secrets. You have my word." His Adam's apple bobbed as he swallowed hard. He locked his fingers around her arms. He stepped in close, his heat tunneling through her thin tank top and deep into her still-sore muscles. "I'll never hurt, betray or disappoint you ever again. I want us to last. No matter how hard things get, I have always and will always need you in my life. I'll spend as long as it takes to prove you can trust me again."

Sincerity deepened the lines carved into his forehead and at the bridge of his nose. He held her steady when all she wanted to do was collapse into him. He meant every word. His expression, his eyes, his hold on her, they all said he wanted this to work, and for the first time since he'd come back into her life, she believed him.

A weak smile curled one corner of her mouth, and she set her palms against his chest. "I haven't slept since that night. I miss having you there in my bed when the nightmares…"

She closed her eyes.

"You don't have to miss me anymore." He pushed a strand of hair behind her ear, urging her to look at him. "I'll be there. Every night to soothe you back to sleep. Every morning to sprinkle cinnamon over your hot chocolate, even when I think you're crazy for drinking it in the summer. I'll be there to decorate the Christmas tree and build you a snow fort. I'll do anything to have that chance again."

"I live in an apartment. I don't have a yard," she said.

A genuine laugh rumbled through him, and oh, how she missed that sound. Missed him. His heart beat strong under her hands, constant, assuring. She focused on the highest mound of scar tissue beneath his T-shirt, the one identical to hers.

"You say all this now," she said, "but I know you, Declan. Even with amnesia, you ran straight at the first monster until you brought him down. It's in your blood. You might've turned down your dream job, but what if another violent criminal is running rampant in Anchorage? What then?"

"Whatever happens, we'll survive, just like we have for the past year. Together." He lifted his hand to her jaw, bringing her gaze up to meet his. A slow burn simmered in her veins at his touch, and it took everything inside of her not to melt against him. His voice dipped an octave as warmth swirled in his eyes. "I told you when Dominic thought he could take you from me—I'm not going anywhere."

She narrowed her eyes. "Are you sure about this?"

"Yes." Declan dropped his hands to hers. "You and I can officially live out our lives without our house getting shot up."

"Wouldn't that be nice? Maybe then I'd stop getting nasty looks from the garbage man." She surveyed the disaster zone that was supposed to be their living room. Focusing on Declan, she curled her fingers in his shirt collar. He'd saved her life, sacrificed his future for her, promised to be honest and open from now on. He deserved the truth, too.

"During our marriage, you dealt with such horrible things, I didn't want to add to any of it. So I kept everything bottled up until it had nowhere else to go. I can't do that again. No matter what happens, I promise to be honest with you, too."

"Then we have a deal?" he asked. "We'll both be honest with each other and try not to mess this up a second—no, wait—a third time?"

"On one condition." He'd sacrificed so much for her already. She didn't have the right to ask for anything more, but he didn't have to give up his dream job. Not for her.

He lowered his forehead against hers, closing his eyes. He untangled his hands from hers, skimmed her lower back and pressed her closer as though he never intended to let her go. "As long as we're together, I'm in."

"Come work for Blackhawk Security," she said. "With me."

Declan pulled away, eyes on her. "What?"

"We made a good team when we worked the Hunter case together. I think we could do it again. Besides, you're too good of an investigator to quit the serial killer business for good. This city needs you. Blackhawk could use another investigator now that we're expanding." She jerked him toward her. "And I need you close."

"You're serious." Excitement brightened his features.

She ran a hand through his tousled brown hair. They'd survived bullet wounds, arrow wounds and had taken down one of Anchorage's most violent serial killers. Together. She could only imagine the possibilities in their future. "I don't want you to resent me down the road. You saved my life, and I know how much that job meant to you. The least I could do is return the favor."

He crushed his lips to hers, penetrating the seam of her mouth with his tongue and thrusting inside. Planting a hand on the back of her head, he seemed intent on making them one. He spread hair-raising pleasure throughout her system. She'd missed his touch, his taste, his warmth. Missed him. He bowed her back into him, her hips level with his.

Her phone pinged from the dresser, and she tore her mouth from his. A reminder. Was it time already? Reaching for her phone, she swiped the reminder off the screen before he had a chance to read it. Yep, right on time. "Besides, Blackhawk will need someone with your particular skill set in a few months when I put in my notice."

She curled her fingers into fists. Why was she so nervous?

"What? It's not the arrow wound, is it?" His hand slipped to her shoulder.

"No, it's not the wound. My injury is healing fine. This is…something else." Kate untangled herself from his arms. He had the right to know. Getting rid of him wasn't going to be easy anyway. Not with that suspicious look on his face. She inhaled deep. "I'm pregnant."

His bottom lip dropped, then his eyes crinkled at the edges. Tension spread from his shoulders down to his toes. A new kind of brightness engulfed his blue eyes. "What? How…how—"

"Are you asking me how we made a baby?" She couldn't read past his shock. Was he excited? Terrified? Both? "Because that should've been something we discussed before we slept together in the snow fort you built in Vincent's backyard. Which we're never going to tell him about."

"No. I remember that very clearly." A smile tugged at the corners of his mouth. He slid his hands around her hips. His warmth permeated her clothing and soothed the bubble of nervousness spreading through her. Mouth a mere inch from hers, he asked, "How far along?"

"Almost six weeks, and I have my very first appointment with the doctor in thirty minutes if you want to come." But Declan still hadn't shown any kind of sign of what was going on inside his head. Nervous energy built behind her sternum. "Okay, you're going to have to tell me what you're thinking. I can't read you right now."

"This is the best day of my life." He pulled her to him and set his mouth against hers once again. "When do we need to leave?"

Heat flooded her system with every pass of his mouth over hers. Wave after wave of blistering arousal swamped her thoughts. She threaded her fingers in his hair at the back of his neck. Not close enough. Dropping her hands to the hem of his shirt, she stepped out of his arms and tugged his shirt over his head.

Deep purple bruising surrounded the bullet wound in his side, but the injury itself had sealed shut. Her insides burned for him. Her husband. Her partner. The love of her life.

"I think we've got enough time to see if the water's been turned back on in the shower first."

* * * * *

Look for The Line of Duty,
*the next Blackhawk Security title
by Nichole Severn, available next month
wherever Harlequin Intrigue books are sold.
Read on for more thrilling suspense!*

He had a lead.

The partial fingerprint he'd lifted from the murder scene hadn't been a partial at all, but evidence of a severe burn on the owner's index finger that tampered with the print. He hadn't been able to get an ID with so few markers to compare before leaving New York City a year ago. But now Blackhawk Security forensic expert Vincent Kalani finally had a chance to bring down a killer.

He hauled his duffel bag highcr on his shoulder. He had to get back to New York, convince his former commanding officer to reopen the case. His muscles burned under the weight as he ducked beneath the small passenger plane's wing and climbed inside. Cold Alaskan air drove beneath his heavy coat but catching sight of the second passenger already aboard chased back the chill.

"Shea Ramsey." Long, curly dark hair slid over her shoulder as jade green eyes widened in surprise. His entire body nearly gave in to the increased sense of gravity pulling at him had it not been for the paralysis working through his muscles. Officer Shea Ramsey had assisted Blackhawk Security with investigations in the past at the insistence of Anchorage's chief of police, but her form-fitting jeans, T-shirt and zip-up hoodie announced she wasn't here on business. Hell, she was a damn beautiful woman, an even better investigator and apparently headed to New York. Same as him. "Anchorage police department's finest, indeed."

"What the hell are you doing here?" Shea shuffled her small backpack at her feet, crossing her arms over her midsection. The tendons between her shoulders and neck corded with tension as she stared out her side of the plane. No mistaking the bitterness in her voice. "Is Blackhawk following me now?"

"Should we be?" Blackhawk Security provided top-of-the-line security measures for their exclusive clientele, including cameras, body-heat sensors, motion detectors and more. Whatever their clients needed, Sullivan Bishop and his team delivered: personal protection, network security, private investigating, logistical support to the US government and personal recovery. They even had their very own profiler on staff to aid the FBI with serial cases. The firm did it all. Vincent mainly headed the forensics division, but he'd take up any case with Shea's involvement in a heartbeat. His gut tightened. Hard to ignore the quiet strength she kept close to the vest when they'd partnered together on these last few cases. It'd pulled him in, made him want to get to know her more, but she'd only met him—and every member of his team—with resentment. Not all Anchorage PD officers agreed with the partnership between the city and the most prestigious security firm in Alaska. And Officer Ramsey led the charge.

He shoved his duffel into the cargo area as the pilot maneuvered into his seat. The small plane bounced with the movement, pushing her scent toward him. Something…grounding. Earthy. "I'm not here on Blackhawk business. I've got…personal business to take care of in New York. You?"

"I have a life outside of the department." She hadn't turned to look at him, her knuckles white through the thin skin of her hands as she gripped the seat's arms. The plane's engine growled at the push of a button, rotors sending vibrations through the tiny sardine jar meant to get them to New York in one piece.

"You guys ready?" the pilot asked. "Here are your headsets."

Hell, Shea was so tense as she took hers, she probably thought the wrong gust of wind could shoot them out of the sky. She closed her eyes, muscles working hard in her throat. The tarmac attendants removed the heavy wooden blocks from around the plane's wheels, and they slowly rolled forward. Every muscle down her spine seemed to tighten.

And something inside him broke for her, forced him to reach out. Vincent positioned the headset over his ears then slid his hand on top of hers.

Smooth skin caught on the calluses in his palms, and suddenly those green eyes were on him. In an instant, her fingers tangled with his. Heat exploded through him, the breath rushing out of his lungs as she gripped onto him as though her life depended on it.

Pressure built behind his sternum as the small passenger plane raced down the runway then climbed high into the sky. His back pressed into the soft leather seats, but his attention focused 100 percent on the woman beside him. On the way her veins tried to escape the translucent skin of her forearm, the unsteady rising and falling of her shoulders when she breathed. Snow-capped Chugach mountains disappeared below the windows, only reappearing as the plane leveled out high above the peaks mere minutes later. The pilot directed them toward the mountains, but the pressure still hadn't released from his rib cage. Not when Shea was still holding on to him so tightly. He raised his voice over the sound of the engine. "I'm going to need that hand back sooner or later."

"Right. Sorry." Shea released her grip then wiped her palm down her thigh, running the same hand through her curly hair. Her voice barely registered above the noise around them. "You'd think five years on the job would give me a little more backbone when it came to planes."

"There's a difference between facing the bad guys and facing our fears." His hand was still warm from where their skin had contact, and he curled his fingers into his palm to hold on to it for as long as he could. "At least there was for me."

She slid that beautiful gaze to his, the freckles dusted across the bridge of her nose and onto her cheeks more pronounced than a few minutes ago. "You were with the NYPD's forensics unit for nine years before you came out here, right? Can't imagine there's much that scares you anymore."

She'd be surprised. Her words slowly registered over the engine's midfrequency drone, and Vincent narrowed his attention. She'd looked into him. There was no way she could've known how long he'd worked forensics by simply searching for him on the internet. NYPD records weren't public information. Which meant she'd used her access through federal databases. Out of curiosity? Or something else? His attention darted to his duffel bag. He'd booked a private passenger plane out of Merrill Field airport for a reason. The Sig Sauer P226 with twelve deadly rounds of ammo in the magazine was currently nestled in his bag. He'd worked with Officer Ramsey before. The background check the firm had run on her when Blackhawk had need of the department's assistance on past investigations hadn't connected her with anyone from his past. But what were the chances that she of all people had ended up on this flight? "Someone's been doing their homework."

"All of you Blackhawk Security types are the same. You take the law into your own hands and don't care if you jeopardize the department's cases.

You run your own investigations then expect officers like me to take clean up your mess. You are vigilantes, and you endanger the people in this city every time you step out of your downtown high-rise office. So, yes, I've done my homework. I like to know who I'm being forced to work with." She pinned him to his seat with that green gaze, and the world disappeared around them. "And you... you were a cop. You used to have a conscience."

Vincent clenched his back teeth against the fire exploding through him. He leaned toward her, ensuring she couldn't look away this time. "You have no idea—"

The plane jerked downward, throwing his heart into his throat. The engine choked then started up again. He locked his attention out through the plane's windshield. His pulse beat loud behind his ears. The rotors were slowing, making them easy to follow. He shouldn't have been able to track a single propeller if they were going the right speed. Gripping one hand around his seat's arm, he pressed his shoulders into the leather and shouted into his mic. "What the hell is going on?"

"I don't know." The pilot shot his hand to the instrument panel. "We're losing altitude fast, but all of the gauges check out." Wrapping his hand around the plane's handheld CB radio, the pilot raised his voice over the protests of the engine. "Mayday, Mayday, Mayday. Merrill Field, this is Captain Reginald, a Robin DR400, Delta-Echo, Lima, Juliet, Golf with total engine failure attempting forced landing. Last known position seven miles east of Anchorage, 1,500 feet heading ninety degrees." Static filled their headsets. "Can anybody read me?" The pilot looked back at his passengers. "The controls aren't responding. I'm going to have to try to put her down manually!"

Vincent pressed his hand to the window and searched the ridges and valleys below for a safe place they could land. Nothing but pure white snow and miles of mountains. Jagged peaks, trees. There was no way they'd survive a forced landing here. There were no safe places to land.

"No, no, no, no. This wasn't supposed to happen." The panic in Shea's voice flooded his veins with ice. She grabbed her backpack off the floor from between her feet and clutched it to her chest. Fear showed brightly in those green eyes a split second before she was thrown back in her seat. She clutched the window. "This wasn't supposed to happen."

The engine smoked, and the plane jerked again. Vincent slammed into the side door. Pain ricocheted through the side of his head, but he forced it to the back of his mind. They were losing altitude too fast, dizziness gripping him hard. They had to get the engine back up and running, or they were all going to die. He couldn't breathe. Couldn't think. Double-checking his seat belt, Vincent locked on Shea's terrified features. The mountain directly outside her window edged closer. "Watch out!"

Metal met rock in an ear-piercing screech. The mountain face cut into the side of the plane, taking the right wing, then caught on the back stabilizer and ripped off the tail end. Cold Alaska air rushed into the cabin as luggage and supplies vanished into the wilderness. The plane rocked to one side, the ground coming up to meet them faster than Vincent expected. He dug his fingers into the leather armrest, every muscle in his body tight.

The pilot's voice echoed through the cabin. "Brace for impact!"

He reached out for Shea. "Hang on!"

THE SKY WAS on fire.

Red streaks bled into purple on one side and green on the other as she stared out the small window to her right, stars prickling through the Auroras she'd fallen in love with the very first night she'd come to Anchorage. Rocky peaks and trees framed her vision, and every cell in her body flooded with pain in an instant. A groan caught in Shea's throat, the weight on her chest blocking precious oxygen. Her feet were numb. How long had she been unconscious? Her hands shook as she tested the copilot seat weighing on her sternum. Closing her eyes against the agony, she put everything she had into getting out from under the hunk of metal and leather, but it wouldn't budge.

The plane had gone down, Vincent's shout so loud in her head. And then... Shea pushed at the debris again as panic clawed through her. They'd crashed in the mountains. The pilot hadn't been able to reach anyone on the radio. Did anyone even know they were out here? She couldn't breathe. Tears burned at the corners of her eyes as the remains of the plane came into focus. Along with the unconscious man in the seat beside her. "Vincent, can you hear me?"

His long black hair covered the pattern of tattoos inked into his arms and neck as well as his overly attractive face. His Hawaiian heritage and that body of a powerful demigod had tugged at something primal within her every time she'd been forced to work alongside him in the field, but she'd buried that feeling deep. He shouldn't have been here. The pilot had told her she'd be the only passenger on this flight. She hadn't meant for the Blackhawk Security operative to get involved—hadn't meant anyone to get involved—but she'd been so desperate to get to New York. That same desperation tore through her now as the plane jerked a few more inches along the snowbank. Out Vincent's window, it looked like they'd crashed at the base of one of the mountains, with nothing but sky and snow past a cliff's edge. A scream escaped her throat as the cabin shook. Any wrong movement would send them down the short slope and over the edge.

"Shea." A groan reached her ears as Vincent stirred in his seat. Locking soothing brown eyes on her though the trail of blood snaking through his left eyebrow, he pushed his hair back with one hand. "That…did not go as I expected. It's going to be okay. We're going to be okay."

Was he trying to convince her or himself?

"I can't...breathe." Understanding lit his bearded features as he noted the seat pressing against her chest, and in that moment, she tensed against the concern sliding into his expression. The memory of him holding her hand during takeoff rushed to the front of her mind. Vincent pushed out of his seat, and the plane slid another couple of inches toward the cliff. She closed her eyes as terror lightninged through her. "No, don't!"

"Shea, look at me." His featherlight touch trailed down her jaw, and she forced herself to follow his command. He stilled, bending at the knees until her gaze settled on his. Her heart pounded hard at the base of her skull but slowed the longer he stared at her. "I'm going to get you out of here, okay? You have my word. I need you to trust me."

Trust him. The people he worked for—worked with—couldn't be trusted. None of them could. Blackhawk Security might help catch the bad guys, same as her, but at the cost of breaking the law she'd taken an oath to uphold. They didn't deserve her trust, but the pressure behind her sternum wouldn't let up, was getting worse, and all she could do was nod against the pain.

He moved forward slowly, and Shea strengthened her grip on the metal crushing her chest. The only reason the seat hadn't killed her was because of the padded backpack she'd clutched before the crash, but how much more could her body take? The plane was shifting again, threatening to slide right toward the cliff. They'd survived a crash landing from 1,500 feet. What were the chances they'd survive another? Vincent crouched beside her, the plane barely large enough to contain his hulking size. Although the gaping hole at the tail end helped. "Hey, eyes on me, Officer. Nowhere else, you got that? I'm going to try to get this thing off you, but I need you to focus on me."

Focus on him. She could do that. She'd spent so long trying to not notice him while they worked their joint investigation, it was a nice change to have permission for once. Pins and needles spread through her feet and hands as cold worked deep into her bones. The back of the plane had been separated from the main fuselage, and the bloodied windshield had a large hole where she'd expected to see the pilot in his seat. They were in the middle of the Alaskan wilderness and temperatures were dropping by the minute. "You're…bleeding."

"I've survived worse." He skimmed his fingers over hers, and her awareness of how close he'd gotten rocketed her heart into her throat.

"Worse than…a plane crash?" How was that possible? She'd read his service records, thanks to a former partner now working for the NYPD. Vincent Kalani had been assigned to the department's detective forensic investigations division, collecting and analyzing evidence from crime scenes for close to ten years. Until suddenly he wasn't. There was nothing in those files about an injury in the line of duty. In fact, it was as though he'd simply disappeared before signing on with Sullivan Bishop's new security firm here in Anchorage.

"I think I've got this loose enough to move it. You ready? I need you to push the seat forward as hard as you can." Vincent handled the leather seat crushing her chest. "On my count. One, two, three." Together, they shoved the debris forward, and Shea gasped as much crisp, clean air as her lungs allowed.

"Thank you." The pressure vanished as he maneuvered the hunk of metal to the front of the plane, and a hysterical laugh bubbled to the surface. Because if she didn't have this small release, Shea feared she might break down here in front of him. The ground rumbled beneath them, and she stilled. The plane hadn't moved. At least, not as far as she could tell. So what—

Another shock wave rolled through the fuselage, and she tightened her grip around the backpack in her lap. "Vincent…"

Fear cut through the relief that'd spread over his expression. "Avalanche."

Shea twisted in her seat, staring up at the ripples creasing through the snowbanks high above, her fingers plastered against the window. Strong hands ripped her out of her seat and thrust her toward the back of the plane. Adrenaline dumped into her veins, triggering her fight-or-flight response. The plane tilted to one side as they raced toward the back, threatening to roll with their escape. Cargo slid into her path. Her boot caught on a black duffel bag, and she hit freezing metal. The rumble was growing louder outside, stronger.

"Go, go, go!" Vincent helped her to her feet, keeping close on her heels as the plane shifted beneath them. With a final push, he forced her through the hole where the tail end of the plane was supposed to be, but they couldn't stop. Not with an entire mountain of snow cascading directly toward them.

Snow worked into the tops of her boots and soaked through her jeans. She pumped her legs as hard as she could, but it wouldn't be enough. The avalanche was moving too fast. She was going to die out here, and everything she'd worked for—everything she'd ever cared about—wouldn't matter anymore.

"There!" Vincent fisted her jacket and wrenched her ahead of him. "Head for that opening!"

Trying to gain control of the panic eating her alive from the inside, Shea sprinted as fast as several feet of snow would let her toward what looked like the entrance to a cave a mere twenty feet ahead of them. Her fingers ached from the grip she kept on the backpack, but it was nothing compared to the burn in her lungs. A rush of cold air and flecks of snow blew her hair into her face and disrupted her vision, but she wouldn't stop. Couldn't. Ten feet. Five. She swung her free arm to gain momentum. Sweat beaded at the base of her spine. They were going to make it. They had to make it. Glancing back over her shoulder, she ensured Vincent was still behind her, but the plane had already been consumed. Snow started to fall over the cave's entrance in a thundering rush, and she lunged for the opening before it disappeared completely.

And hit solid dirt.

She clutched the backpack close to her chest, as if it'd bring any kind of comfort.

Within seconds, darkness filled her vision, only the sound of her and Vincent's combined breathing registering over the low sound of them being buried alive. She reached for him, skimming her fingertips across what she assumed was one of his arms, but the padding of his jacket was too thick to be sure. Dust filled her nostrils as she fought to catch her breath. Silence descended, the wall of snow and ice settling over the cave. "You saved my life."

A soft hissing sound preceded a burst of orange flame. Shadows danced over Vincent's features, his battle-worn expression on full display in the dull flicker of the lighter, and a hint of the awareness she'd felt when he'd held her hand during takeoff settled low in her stomach. Faster than she thought possible, he hauled her from the floor and pinned her against the wall of the cave and his body with one hand, her pack forgotten. "Tell me why you were on that plane."

His body pressed into hers. Shadowed, angry angles carved into his features, unlike anything she'd seen before when they'd worked together. Shea pushed at him, but he was so much stronger, so much bigger. "Get off me."

"Before we crashed you said, 'This wasn't supposed to happen.'" He increased the pressure at the base of her throat, simulating the crushing debris he'd pulled off her chest mere minutes ago. "There was no reason that plane should've crashed unless it'd been sabotaged. You know something, and I'm not letting you go until you tell me who sent you after me—"

Turning one side of her body into him, she struck his forearm with the base of her palm and withdrew her service weapon with her free hand from the shoulder holster beneath her jacket. She aimed center mass, just as she'd been trained, but kept her finger alongside the trigger. "Touch me again and I won't hesitate to shoot you. Understand?" He backed off, easing the flood of blood pulsing in her face and neck. "Nobody sent me after you, whatever the hell that means." In the dim light of the flame, Shea swallowed the discomfort in her throat as though that'd make it easier to breathe but wouldn't lower her weapon. "I was on the plane because I need to get my son back."

***

Don't miss
The Line Of Duty *by Nichole Severn,*
available October 2020 wherever
Harlequin Intrigue books and ebooks are sold.
www.Harlequin.com

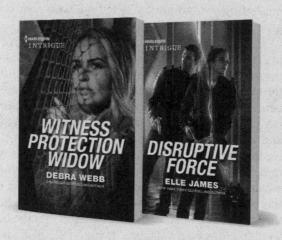

COMING NEXT MONTH FROM

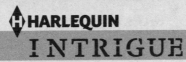

INTRIGUE

Available September 15, 2020

#1953 SUSPICIOUS CIRCUMSTANCES
A Badge of Honor Mystery • by Rita Herron
Special agent Liam Maverick asks for nurse Peyton Weiss's help in his hunt for the person who caused the hospital fire that killed his father. But someone doesn't want Peyton to share what she knows...and they'll do whatever it takes to keep her quiet.

#1954 TEXAS KIDNAPPING
An O'Connor Family Mystery • by Barb Han
After stopping a would-be kidnapper from taking her newly adopted daughter, Renee Smith accepts US Marshal Cash O'Connor's offer of a safe haven at his Texas ranch. The case resembles his sister's unsolved kidnapping thirty years ago, and Cash won't allow history to repeat itself.

#1955 THE LINE OF DUTY
Blackhawk Security • by Nichole Severn
When Blackhawk operative Vincent Kalani boarded an airplane, he never expected it to crash into the Alaskan mountains, but by-the-book police officer Shea Ramsey soon becomes his unlikely partner in survival. Can they escape the wilderness, or will their attackers find them first?

#1956 MARINE PROTECTOR
Fortress Defense • by Julie Anne Lindsey
Pursued by a madman, single mom Lyndy Wells and her infant son are bodyguard Cade Lance's priority assignment. Cade knows they must find the serial killer quickly or Lyndy and her baby will face grave danger. And Cade won't let that happen on his watch.

#1957 WITNESS SECURITY BREACH
A Hard Core Justice Thriller • by Juno Rushdan
There's not a target out there that US Marshals Aiden Yazzie and Charlotte "Charlie" Killinger can't bring down. Until a high-profile witness goes missing and a fellow marshal is murdered. Can they steer clear of temptation to find their witness before it's too late?

#1958 STALKED IN THE NIGHT
by Carla Cassidy
The target of a brutal criminal, Eva Martin is determined to defend her son and her ranch. Jake Albright is a complication she doesn't need—especially since he doesn't know about their child. As danger escalates and a shared desire grows, can Eva hold on to the family she's just regained?

HICNM0920

SPECIAL EXCERPT FROM

(H) HARLEQUIN

INTRIGUE

*When Blackhawk operative Vincent Kalani boarded
an airplane, he never expected it to crash into the
Alaskan mountains, but by-the-book police officer
Shea Ramsey soon becomes his unlikely partner in
survival. Can they escape the wilderness, or will
their attackers find them first?*

Read on for a sneak preview of
The Line of Duty *by Nichole Severn.*

He had a lead.

The partial fingerprint he'd lifted from the murder
scene hadn't been a partial at all, but evidence of a severe
burn on the owner's index finger that altered the print.
He hadn't been able to get an ID with so few markers to
compare before leaving New York City a year ago. But
now, Blackhawk Security forensic expert Vincent Kalani
finally had a chance to bring down a killer.

He hauled his duffel bag higher on his shoulder.
He had to get back to New York, convince his former
commanding officer to reopen the case. His muscles
burned under the weight as he ducked beneath the small
passenger plane's wing and climbed inside. Cold Alaskan
air drove beneath his heavy coat, but catching sight of the
second passenger already aboard chased back the chill.

HIEXP0920

"Shea Ramsey." Long, curly dark hair slid over her shoulder as jade-green eyes widened in surprise. His entire body nearly gave in to the increased sense of gravity pulling at him had it not been for the paralysis working through his muscles. Officer Shea Ramsey had assisted Blackhawk Security with investigations in the past at the insistence of Anchorage's chief of police, but her form-fitting pair of jeans, T-shirt and zip-up hoodie announced she wasn't here on business. Hell, she was a damn beautiful woman, an even better investigator and apparently headed to New York. Same as him. "Anchorage Police Department's finest, indeed."

"What the hell are you doing here?" Shea shuffled her small backpack at her feet, crossing her arms over her midsection. The tendons between her shoulders and neck corded with tension as she stared out her side of the plane. No mistaking the bitterness in her voice. "Is Blackhawk following me now?"

"Should we be?"

Don't miss
The Line of Duty *by Nichole Severn,*
available October 2020 wherever
Harlequin Intrigue books and ebooks are sold.

Harlequin.com

HIEXP0920

Get 4 FREE REWARDS!

We'll send you 2 FREE Books plus 2 FREE Mystery Gifts.

WHAT SHE DID
BARB HAN
LARGER PRINT

HOSTILE PURSUIT
JUNO RUSHDAN
LARGER PRINT

Harlequin Intrigue books are action-packed stories that will keep you on the edge of your seat. Solve the crime and deliver justice at all costs.

FREE
Value Over
$20

YES! Please send me 2 FREE Harlequin Intrigue novels and my 2 FREE gifts (gifts are worth about $10 retail). After receiving them, if I don't wish to receive any more books, I can return the shipping statement marked "cancel." If I don't cancel, I will receive 6 brand-new novels every month and be billed just $4.99 each for the regular-print edition or $5.99 each for the larger-print edition in the U.S., or $5.74 each for the regular-print edition or $6.49 each for the larger-print edition in Canada. That's a savings of at least 12% off the cover price! It's quite a bargain! Shipping and handling is just 50¢ per book in the U.S. and $1.25 per book in Canada.* I understand that accepting the 2 free books and gifts places me under no obligation to buy anything. I can always return a shipment and cancel at any time. The free books and gifts are mine to keep no matter what I decide.

Choose one:
☐ **Harlequin Intrigue**
   Regular-Print
   (182/382 HDN GNXC)

☐ **Harlequin Intrigue**
   Larger-Print
   (199/399 HDN GNXC)

Name (please print)

Address _____ Apt. #

City _____ State/Province _____ Zip/Postal Code

Email: Please check this box ☐ if you would like to receive newsletters and promotional emails from Harlequin Enterprises ULC and its affiliates. You can unsubscribe anytime.

> **Mail to the Reader Service:**
> **IN U.S.A.:** P.O. Box 1341, Buffalo, NY 14240-8531
> **IN CANADA:** P.O. Box 603, Fort Erie, Ontario L2A 5X3

Want to try 2 free books from another series! Call 1-800-873-8635 or visit www.ReaderService.com.

---

*Terms and prices subject to change without notice. Prices do not include sales taxes, which will be charged (if applicable) based on your state or country of residence. Canadian residents will be charged applicable taxes. Offer not valid in Quebec. This offer is limited to one order per household. Books received may not be as shown. Not valid for current subscribers to Harlequin Intrigue books. All orders subject to approval. Credit or debit balances in a customer's account(s) may be offset by any other outstanding balance owed by or to the customer. Please allow 4 to 6 weeks for delivery. Offer available while quantities last.

Your Privacy—Your information is being collected by Harlequin Enterprises ULC, operating as Reader Service. For a complete summary of the information we collect, how we use this information and to whom it is disclosed, please visit our privacy notice located at corporate.harlequin.com/privacy-notice. From time to time we may also exchange your personal information with reputable third parties. If you wish to opt out of this sharing of your personal information, please visit readerservice.com/consumerchoice or call 1-800-873-8635. **Notice to California Residents**—Under California law, you have specific rights to control and access your data. For more information on these rights and how to exercise them, visit corporate.harlequin.com/california-privacy.

HI20R2

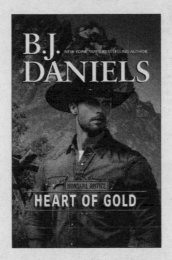

Love Harlequin romance?

DISCOVER.

Be the first to find out about promotions, news and exclusive content!

f Facebook.com/HarlequinBooks

🐦 Twitter.com/HarlequinBooks

📷 Instagram.com/HarlequinBooks

📌 Pinterest.com/HarlequinBooks

ReaderService.com

EXPLORE.

Sign up for the Harlequin e-newsletter and download a free book from any series at **TryHarlequin.com**

CONNECT.

Join our Harlequin community to share your thoughts and connect with other romance readers!
Facebook.com/groups/HarlequinConnection